READERS ARE SAYING...

The Story Jar

... isn't just for Mother's Day—if you are a mother, have a mother, or would like to be a mother, this book is for you.

... a story about an ordinary jar that holds an extraordinary power to encourage and heal the heart.

Perfect! . . . I found myself near tears of sadness at times, joy at others, and a few times a feeling of awe and wonder that only another mother could understand.

Lovely! You won't be disappointed in these tender stories of motherhood.

A beautiful tribute to motherhood—great for gift-giving . . . real, painful, hopeful.

... this book has touched me more than any other I have read. I cried, I laughed, and I relearned things that I had forgotten long ago. . . . I plan on giving it to all the "mothers" in my life for Mother's Day.

The
STORY JAR
a novel

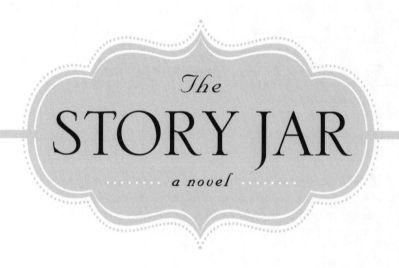

The
STORY JAR

a novel

ROBIN LEE HATCHER &
DEBORAH BEDFORD

HENDRICKSON
PUBLISHERS

The Story Jar

Hendrickson Publishers Marketing, LLC
P. O. Box 3473
Peabody, Massachusetts 01961-3473

ISBN 978-1-59856-665-9

The 2011 edition of *The Story Jar,* Hendrickson Publishers, by arrangement with copyright holders from the original edition, published 2001 by Multnomah Publishers.

Deborah Bedford © 2011 *The Hair Ribbons*
Robin Lee Hatcher © 2011 *Heart Rings*

All scripture quotations, unless otherwise indicated, are taken from the Holy Bible, New International Version®, NIV®. Copyright ©1973, 1978, 1984 by Biblica, Inc.™ Used by permission of Zondervan. All rights reserved worldwide. www.zondervan.com

Cover Photo Credit: Kindler, Andreas, Getty Images

Printed in the United States of America

First Printing Hendrickson Publishers Edition — April 2011

CONTENTS

Afterwords:

THE STORY BEHIND *The Story Jar*

by

ROBIN LEE HATCHER

In September 1998, I received a story jar as a thank you gift after speaking at a writers' conference in Nebraska. The small mason jar, the lid covered with a pretty handkerchief, was filled with many odds and ends—a Gerber baby spoon, an empty thread spindle, a colorful pen, several buttons, a tiny American flag, an earring, and more.

The idea behind this gift was a simple one. When a writer can't think of anything to write, she stares at one of the objects in the jar and lets her imagination play. Who did that belong to? How old was he? What sort of person was he? What does the object represent in his life?

Writers love to play the "what if" game. It's how most stories come into being. Something piques their interest, they start asking questions, and a book is born.

A week after receiving my story jar, I attended a retreat with several writer friends of mine, Deborah Bedford included. On the flight home, I told Deborah about the jar. The next thing you know (after all, what better thing is there for writers to do on a plane than play "what if"?), we began brainstorming what would ultimately become

The Story Jar. We decided very quickly that we wanted this to be a book that celebrates motherhood, that encourages mothers, that recognizes how much they should be loved and honored.

The Story Jar was first published by Multnomah in 2001, but eventually went out of print. Thus Deborah and I are delighted that Hendrickson Publishers wanted to bring it out in a new, revised version because we believe these stories can inspire others, just as it did this reader back in 2001:

"I am an avid book reader and have read thousands of books— maybe more—since the age of five. I can honestly say that [*The Story Jar*] has touched me more than any other I have read. I cried, I laughed, and I relearned things that I had forgotten long ago as well as realizing things I never knew. Thank you for sharing your stories with your readers. They are truly inspiring. I plan on giving it to all the 'mothers' in my life for Mother's Day."

You don't have to be a writer to want a story jar. It can be a family's way of preserving memories. Consider having a family get-together where everybody brings an item to go into the jar, and as it drops in, they tell what it means to them, what it symbolizes. We can learn something new about our loved ones when we hear their memories in their own words. Or do what my church did a number of years ago to create a memory for a retiring pastor. Inspired by *The Story Jar*, members of the congregation brought items to the retirement dinner to put into a story jar or they simply wrote their memories on a piece of paper to go into the jar. It was our way of saying thanks to a man and wife for all of the years they'd given in God's service.

A story jar can be a tool for remembering all the wonderful things God has done in our own lives. As Mrs. Halley said, not all of God's miracles are in the Bible. He is still performing them today in countless ways today, changing lives, healing hearts.

In the grip of his grace,
Robin Lee Hatcher

The Story Jar

A Sanctuary

Beth Williams paused in the vestibule, ran her hand over the small wooden table against the wall, then crinkled her nose. The woman who'd called promised the job would be easy, no more than a half day's work. But a solid line of dust marked Beth's palm and fingertips, and the interior of the church probably wasn't in much better shape.

"'Just a light sprucing up for the new pastor,'" Beth mimicked, plopping her pail of supplies on the floor next to the table. "'Only a few hours' work,' the woman said. 'After all, how dirty can a church be?'"

Mrs. Vinci, chairman of the Ladies' Auxiliary in charge of such items, obviously hadn't spent much time cleaning her church. Beth regularly cleaned the Baptist facility on Main Street and the Methodist place on Fourth, and she knew that bubble gum tended to sprout from the underside of church pews. She knew that teenagers tended to hide their angst-filled notes among the pages of hymnals, and that every book in the back six rows would have to be lifted, dusted, and fanned to remove extra-curricular reading material—or gum wrappers—that might offend the sensibilities of a future worshiper.

Sighing, she pulled out a clean dust cloth and a can of furniture polish from her pail. Better to start at the rear of the building and work forward, saving the easy work for last. Folks who sat up front tended to mind their manners more than people in the back—they were neater, at any rate.

She pushed through the double swinging doors and took in the sanctuary with one glance. This little church was brighter than most, with ivory-colored pews instead of the traditional dark mahogany. Sunlight streamed through wide windows, glinting off swirling dust motes in the slanted light. The faint scent of carnations hung in the air.

Up front, Beth noticed, an organ and piano faced off from opposite sides of a platform centered by a small lectern leaning slightly to the right. She finished her perusal and felt one corner of her mouth lift in a wry smile. Someone here—either the pastor or his people, maybe both—appreciated simplicity. There were no ornate carvings or wall hangings, no carved seats or tables, no elevated pulpit. Just two worn wing chairs bracketing the leaning tower of preaching.

She shrugged. All the better. Simple things were easier to dust.

She began at the rear of the sanctuary, pulling folded bulletins from hymnals and tucking them into the plastic bag hanging from her belt. She hummed as she ran her dust cloth over the pews. She began thinking about the last time she'd taken her boys to church. They'd been small then, barely six and eight. But Tommy had pulled another kid's hair in the Sunday school class. When the teacher couldn't wait to tell Beth, she decided her kids didn't need scoldings on Sunday too. She could barely manage to keep up with them Monday through Saturday, so if a Sunday school teacher couldn't get them to mind, she'd just keep them at home.

She bent forward to pick up a forgotten card from a funeral service. She looked at the date and frowned. Just yesterday. No wonder the place smelled like flowers.

A door opened behind her, and Beth glanced over her shoulder at a petite white-haired lady entering the sanctuary. She moved forward with a confident tread and nodded at Beth.

"Don't mind me," the woman said, gesturing toward the front. "I'm just going to sit awhile, if you don't mind."

Beth nodded, though she felt a little foolish. She certainly had no authority here—she didn't even attend this church. She'd have to clean around the woman when she reached the front, but that was certainly no big deal.

The lady slipped into the second pew and sat next to the aisle, her gaze lifting toward the simple pulpit. Beth caught herself glancing at the lectern too, half-expecting someone to miraculously appear behind it. What was the woman doing? Was she senile?

For nearly twenty minutes Beth worked, and all that time the little lady sat without making a sound, her eyes fixed upon the platform, her mouth curved in a sweet smile. Finally, as Beth entered the row immediately behind the woman, she dared to speak: "Are you . . . well, are you all right?"

The lady nodded her head slightly, then threw Beth a guilty smile. "I'm fine. I was just . . . visiting. My husband was the pastor here, you see, until the Lord called him home."

Beth lowered her gaze. "I'm sorry."

The lady smiled again. "Don't be. John was eager for heaven, though I know he regretted leaving this church. And I know he regretted leaving . . . me."

The last word came out in a whisper Beth strained to hear. Then she put the pieces together. After twelve years of faithful service at this church, yesterday Reverend John Halley had been memorialized and buried, she had read on the funeral bulletin now in the plastic bag.

She looked at the woman. "You must be Mrs. Halley."

The woman inclined her head. "I am."

"I'm Beth. Beth Williams."

Suddenly at a loss, Beth sprayed the back of the pew with polish. What was she supposed to say next? She'd already used "I'm sorry." Did pastors and their wives have some sort of special arrangement, she wondered as her rag slid over the top railing, in case one went to heaven before the other? Maybe pastors' wives filled their husbands' positions after they passed on, sort of like senators' wives occasionally filled their husbands' seats until the next election. If so, was it appropriate to congratulate the lady? Probably not, with his funeral hardly over.

She swiped at another wet area with her dust cloth, her charm bracelet jingling in the silence. "What will you do now?" she asked, risking a glance at the older woman. "Keep working in the church?"

Mrs. Halley turned, easing into a smile. "Heavens, no. That wouldn't be fair to the new pastor, would it? People would feel torn if I stayed, so it's best I move on. That's why I'm sitting here—just soaking it all in before I go."

Beth moved a step to the right with her cloth. "Where are you going?"

"Florida. Where else?"

Beth chuckled softly as she continued her polishing. "I have a grandmother in Florida. Lives in a condo in St. Petersburg. Eighty-nine and she still drives a car, though I hear she did pull out of the garage last year with the door still down."

Mrs. Halley chuckled too. "I doubt I'll be doing much driving. I'll be staying with my daughter, and her kids are old enough to drive. I'm hoping they'll think it's cool to taxi grandma around."

Beth lifted a brow, but didn't respond. Her own boys, now seventeen and nineteen, would rather undergo oral surgery than drive an older person anywhere. They'd stopped wanting to be seen with her when they hit thirteen, and now she practically had to make an appointment to speak with them. They came and went at all hours, despite her fervent pleas to be home by midnight, and some of the young people they were hanging with weren't what she'd call bright-eyed examples of American youth.

Grabbing the spray can and dust cloth in one hand and holding the pail in the other, Beth nodded to the woman and moved toward the platform. She would come back to dust the first two pews after Mrs. Halley left. It didn't seem very respectful to dust around the lady, and despite that gentle smile, any woman with her husband just one day in the grave couldn't feel much like conversation.

Beth took one deep, weary breath as she climbed the two carpeted steps. Her own husband had been gone fifteen years. She brushed a lock of hair behind her ear. Probably New York or California, some overpopulated place where he could hide in a crowd and spin Cinderella talk to some unsuspecting woman who'd swallow his lies without a second thought . . . just like she had.

Kneeling, she brushed the padded seat of the wing chair with a whisk broom, then turned the cushion over and noticed that the fabric had faded. The regular church custodian obviously hadn't thought to turn the cushion on a regular basis.

"My, would you look at that."

Beth turned to see Mrs. Halley standing in front of the platform, her eyes wide. "I never thought those chairs would fade."

"All fabrics fade, even if there's just a little sunlight in the room." Beth lifted her shoulders in a light shrug. "It's only a matter of time."

The woman's smile held a hint of apology. "I should have seen to the chairs. They were new when we first came to this church, and I should have taken better care of them."

"Not your job," Beth said, running the little broom beneath the cushion. "Whoever usually cleans this place should have—"

"Cleaning was my job." Mrs. Halley's brows lifted, and her gaze ran over the furnishings of the platform. "John preached, I cleaned and taught Sunday school. We're a small church, you see."

Beth's movements slowed as she struggled to imagine this delicate, genteel woman scrubbing the foyer tile on her hands and knees. She didn't look particularly strong, not the type, actually.

"It's a big job for one person," Beth offered. "Most people don't realize how long it can take to clean a big space like this. You have to check the walls for fingerprints, vacuum, and clean out all those hymnals—"

"Those teenagers," Mrs. Halley interrupted, laughing. "They always wondered how I kept up with their little soap operas. I always knew who liked whom, who was ticked off at someone."

"I did find some interesting reading." Beth leaned down to give the area under the chair a sweep, then felt the broom encounter an object.

"What's this?" She bent lower and squinted through the shadows. "There's something under here."

"Under the chair?" Mrs. Halley mounted the platform and leaned down. "Why, I can't imagine—"

"Just a minute." Beth strained forward and reached until she felt the coolness of glass and metal. A moment later she pulled out a medium-sized Mason jar, its lid rusty with age.

"Oh, my!" Mrs. Halley's hand covered her lips. "I thought we'd lost it." She gave a wry chuckle. "I guess I'm not too good in the cleaning department."

Beth sat back on her knees and lifted the jar into the light. Through the glass she glimpsed an odd assortment of objects—a length of blue ribbon, a single silver earring, a tiny hospital identification bracelet, a Polaroid snapshot, a yellow sock that would only fit a baby or a doll. Slowly she turned the jar, the contents shifting and clinking against the glass. If this was some kind of religious object, she couldn't imagine how it was used.

8

She looked up at the pastor's wife. Mrs. Halley was staring at the jar as if it contained a miracle.

"What is it?" Beth asked.

"It—it's the story jar." Mrs. Halley sank into the wing chair and reached out for the jar with trembling hands. Beth gave it to her, then sat back and looped her arms around her knees. The older woman was also turning the jar, and she started to smile at the objects within.

"It's John's story jar," she whispered, setting the container on her lap. "Every year, beginning when we were first married, my husband would invite the mothers of the church—or sometimes members of their families—to come forward on Mother's Day. Instead of honoring them with flowers and such, he asked *them* to honor God with some little memento, some small token of gratitude. As they placed a special item into the jar, she shared the story behind it with the congregation. Then, together with each mother, the body of Christ rejoiced . . . and sometimes sorrowed. But we all felt the power of the shared story. Every year, we could look at the story jar and see the evidence of God's hand at work in our lives."

Beth tilted her head to further study the jar, now seeing items like a theater ticket stub, a smooth pebble, a set of silver keys upon a simple chain.

"All these things," she gestured toward the jar, "came from people in this church?"

"Not all." Mrs. Halley's voice had gone remote with memory. "Some came from churches we pastored years ago. Everywhere we went, we took the story jar with us because we wanted people to know that God is still working in his people's lives. Not all of his miracles are stories in the Bible. Some are found," her hand twisted the rusty lid, "—in here."

As Beth watched, the woman's blue-veined hand reached into the jar and pulled out a winding length of blue ribbon.

"This belonged to Heidi McKinnis," she said, draping the silky strand over her knee. Beth could see where the shiny decoration, wrinkled from many times being tied into someone's hair, had frayed at the edges. "Heidi and her family were traveling through, on their way to a conference where Heidi's mother was a featured speaker. She said she was so excited about the warm weather, after living in all that snow! It was only a couple of years ago, I believe, and summer had come early that year. I know it's sometimes hard for a teenager to stand up and tell how a mother has influenced her faith. It took a long time for Heidi to gather her courage to bring this to the altar. It was so hot the walls were sweating. But nobody was thinking about the weather by the time she finished telling her story."

"What was it?" Beth couldn't stop the question. She hugged her knees to her chest and managed a nonchalant laugh. "I'm the mother of two teenage boys, you see, and—well, I could use a little encouragement these days."

Mrs. Halley smiled, her blue eyes shimmering with light from the wide windows. "It's a long story. Do you want all the details? Or just the abbreviated version?"

"I've got some time, if you do."

"I have nothing *but* time." Mrs. Halley gazed at the window.

"Go ahead. I'd love to hear it." Beth lifted her chin, willing to be drawn into this narrative, wherever it went.

"It all began"—Mrs. Halley ran the ribbon between her fingers as she spoke—"with the annual Christmas production of *The Nutcracker. . . .*"

Part One

THE
HAIR RIBBONS

by

DEBORAH BEDFORD

In memory of Katie Dunlap, beloved sister in Christ, who danced so well before the Lord.

To Tommie, who reminds me as often as we talk what a gift it is to have a mother who, above all things, loves the Father.

Blessed are the pure in heart: for they shall see God. (Matthew 5:8 KJV)

The Nutcracker

In the lower-level community room of The Pink Garter Plaza, the highly anticipated day had finally arrived. Rehearsals would begin for the annual holiday production of *The Nutcracker*.

Party-scene dancers and clowns crowded into dressing rooms, giggling and yanking at ballet slippers now two sizes tight over a summer left in the closet. Angels and mice played boisterous tag, weaving in and out among everyone's legs, around the furniture, under the restroom doors. Little girls all, with their hair finger-combed into haphazard buns, wearing tights with knees that hadn't come quite as clean as they ought, running amok the way little girls run in every hallway in every dance studio in every town.

Behind them came their mothers, towing younger siblings, toting coats and backpacks, handing off crumpled lunch bags smelling of bologna and greasy potato chips and sharp cheese.

"Angels in studio one."

"Pick up a schedule on your way out."

"Mice over here, please."

Instructions nearly impossible to be heard over the cacophony of noise, music, voices in every key, shouts, laughter. The mothers added their own chatter, waving hello to friends as they dodged around one another in the hallway. Several stopped to watch their daughters at warm ups through the one-way mirror.

"We need volunteers!" One of the dance instructors dangled a tape measure in the air. "This may be the only time all year we have all the mice together in one place. We need somebody to take head measurements, to make sure the ears are going to fit."

As often happens with groups of mothers, a small clan of doers collected tape measures and began the tasks at hand, measuring heads, jotting numbers, cheerfully recounting the joys and hassles of other performances of previous years. But after all the hoopla had died down and the actual dancing had begun, only one was left to wait outside the one-way mirror. A mother stood alone, savoring her daughter's every glissade, every pirouette and plié, watching as if she couldn't tear her eyes away.

It wasn't a difficult dance, this dance of the angels. Theia McKinnis knew each of the delicate, careful movements by heart. Heidi, her daughter, had danced the role of angel last year. And the year before. And the year before that.

A door opened across the way and out came Julie Stevens, *The Nutcracker*'s director of performance. "Sorry to keep you waiting," she said briskly, snapping her cell phone shut. "I've been on the telephone. You know what it's like when you get stuck with someone who wants to talk."

Okay, so that's my cue, Theia thought.

Muted from behind the glass, Tchaikovsky's music swelled to its elegant climax before it ebbed away and began again.

"Oh, no. I'm not worried about the time," the woman assured her as Theia glanced at the clock above the studio door. "Come in my office. We'll talk."

When she took a seat inside, Theia folded her arms across her chest as if she felt the need to protect herself from something. She realized at that moment exactly why she'd come. In this one place in her life, she needed to gain control.

"I'm here to talk about Heidi. Her dancing."

"Her dancing in *The Nutcracker*? Right. She's been cast in the role of an angel."

"She's danced as an angel for three years."

A pause. "Do you see that as a problem?"

In this small town, another week would pass and it would be impossible for anybody not to have heard about Theia's cancer. *Of course there is time,* Dr. Sugden had told her in his office when he'd given them the results of the biopsy. *You have plenty of time to seek out a second opinion, if you'd like. I could even recommend somebody. You have plenty of time to educate yourself. You have plenty of time to develop a survival plan.*

Even here in the dance studio, Theia had to fight to keep the panic out of her voice, just thinking about it. *A survival plan.*

"Heidi wants to dance something different this year. She wants to do something more difficult, something that shows she's growing. Growing in skill."

The dance director picked up a roll of breath mints and ran a fingernail around one mint, popping it loose before she peeled the foil back. "Surely you realize we can't jostle everyone around once the girls have been cast."

"I know it might be difficult, but—"

"We can't give every child the part she dreams of, Mrs. McKinnis. If we did that, we'd have thirty girls dancing the part of the Sugar

Plum Fairy and thirty more dancing the role of Marie. Heidi is perfect as our lead angel. Heidi *looks* like an angel."

"She's the oldest one, in the easiest dance."

"She knows the part so well that the younger girls follow her well. That's why we always put her right in the front the way we do." Her eyebrows arched appealingly, but Theia fought back a swirl of emotions, including irritation.

"It is small consolation, positioned on the front row but in a place where you don't want to be."

"Mrs. McKinnis." Julie Stevens crunched her breath mint and didn't reach for another. "I promise that I will make note of this. I promise that I will cast your daughter in a different role next year." She fingered a pen on her desk as if she would write the note immediately.

There isn't any guarantee that I will be here next year.

Heidi didn't even fit into the angel costume anymore. Every year, a volunteer seamstress altered and lengthened the burgundy dress with its hoop skirt and its tinsel halo and its gossamer wings.

Theia laced her fingers together, her hands a perfect plait in her lap that belied the anger rising in her midsection. The only problem was, she didn't know exactly whom to be angry at. At herself, for letting time slip past without stopping to notice? At Julie Stevens, for holding Heidi back and not letting her blossom?

At God, for letting cancer slip into her life when she least expected it?

Theia stood from the chair and didn't smile. A crazy motto from some deodorant commercial played in her mind. "Never let them see you sweat." She clutched her purse in front of her and gave a little shake of her head. "Miss Stevens, there are others who could be your lead angel. Some day maybe you'll realize that a child's heart is more important than the quality of some annual performance."

The teenagers in Jackson Hole, the ones still too young to drive, had gotten their freedom this past summer, a paved bike path that ribboned past meadows and neighborhoods, past the middle school and the new post office, clear up to the northern outskirts of town. Kate McKinnis and her best friend, Jaycee, leaned their mountain bikes against the side of the house, hurried into the kitchen for sodas, and tromped upstairs to Kate's room. Jaycee checked messages on her cell phone while Kate sorted through songs and turned on one of her favorites on the iPod.

"Turn it up." Jaycee flopped on the bed and buttressed her chin against a plush rabbit that happened to be in her way. "I love that song."

"I can't. Today's Saturday. Dad works on his sermons on Saturdays. I have to keep it quiet."

"That reeks."

"On Saturdays, he waits to hear from the Lord. He doesn't want to hear ZOEgirl instead." Kate picked a bottle of chartreuse nail polish and handed it to Jaycee. "I'll do your right hand if you'll do my left."

"Only if I can put it on my toes, too."

"Something's wrong with my dad. He's been quiet for the last week. He isn't laughing much. And neither is Mom."

"Happens with my parents too. Maybe they had a fight."

Kate shook her head. "He's taking her for a picnic when my sister gets back from dancing. I have to babysit her in a little while."

"Can I use purple? Green and purple, back and forth between toes. Do you think that would look stupid?"

"If it does, you can always take it off."

They bent over each other's splayed fingers and toes, accompanied by the constant thrum of the music. Jaycee finished with the purple and screwed on the top. "Did you hear about Megan Spence?

Her parents are letting her drive the car already. She gets her learner's permit now that she's fourteen."

"I want to drive, too. Just imagine what it'll be like, Jaycee. We can go anywhere we want."

"Megan's getting her hardship license or something."

"Not fair." Kate waved her nails in the air to dry them, then pulled her hair back with one hand.

"Let me do that. You'll get smudges." Jaycee grabbed the brush, made a quick ponytail and clipped it with a hair claw so it sprang from Kate's head like a rhododendron. "There."

"How do I look?" Kate surveyed both her hair and her upheld green fingernails in the mirror.

"Like a hottie. Same as me."

"Do you think Sam Hastings is cute?"

"He rocks. But he's got a girlfriend."

"Well, you know, I just like him as a *friend*."

"When I get my license, I'm going to get in the car and just start driving. Just take any road I think looks good." Jaycee started brushing her own hair, too. "Maybe I'll drive all the way to Canada. Or Alaska. Or Mars."

"You can't drive to Mars, silly. There aren't any roads."

"I'll make my own roads. Really, I'll just start out somewhere and take any road I want, without a map or anything. Just to drive forever and see where I'd end up."

"You'd end up lost."

"You can't end up lost, can you, if you don't need to know where you're going?"

- -

It occurred to Joe McKinnis, watching the blanket flutter to the grass, that perhaps he hadn't chosen the best spot for this picnic.

His wife stood at the edge of Flat Creek, protective arms crossed over her bosom, counting swallows as they swooped and dipped under the bridge and over the water. Just the sight of her took his breath away. Her hair, the same color as the cured autumn grasses in the meadow, had gone webby and golden in the sunlight. As she stood at water's edge, she belonged to the countryside around her, the standing pines, the weeds, the wind.

I wonder if the chemo's going to make her lose her hair.

Almost as soon as he asked the question, he berated himself. *That isn't what she needs from you, Joe. She needs you to stand beside her. She needs you to tell her to believe in miracles. She needs you to counsel with her the way you counsel every parishioner who comes to your office seeking answers.*

But this was his own wife he was talking about. For her, he had no answers. At least any that worked.

Joe settled on his knees and called out. "Theia? You ready for lunch?"

"Not quite." She didn't turn when she answered him. "It's such a beautiful place."

"It's pretty, isn't it?"

She started toward him then, her steps rustling like crinoline as she moved through the grass. "Thank you. A picnic was a good idea."

He stood and watched her approach. "We needed to talk."

Theia stopped beside a copse of low-lying willows where a little makeshift cross rested against a pile of rocks. Kate and Heidi had made it last year, lashing together sticks with string to mark their dog's grave.

Even now he heard the girls' voices, their pointed questions full of both hope and sorrow. "Do you think dogs go to heaven when they die, Daddy?"

"Maybe dogs don't have to ask Jesus into their heart, 'cause they aren't people."

"If there's horses in heaven, why can't there be dogs, too?"

Theia resumed her steps. "This was a good place to bury Maggie," she said now. "She loved it here."

Joe reached out a hand and finally voiced it. "Maybe not such a good place to come today." He embraced her quickly, then knelt again to set out their food. Two sandwiches with ham and mustard. Apples. The clear plastic container of brownies.

Theia knelt beside him, unwrapped a sandwich. "Why? Why wouldn't it be a good place?"

"You know, because this is where we"—a little pause—"buried the dog."

She took her first bite but, after a moment, her chewing slowed. "We should pray," she said, her mouth full. But they didn't. She kept right on eating. Joe chomped into his apple, as crisp as the air.

For two people who had so much to say to each other, it seemed strange that nothing would come.

At last when they did speak, they spoke unison.

"Kate knows something is wrong," Joe said.

"Heidi's going to be an angel again." From Theia.

They'd both been stunned, shattered, silent since the night he had accidentally found it. "Theia, there's something—a lump—that hasn't been here before," he whispered afterward. "You ought to have someone take a look at it."

Now, as he sat across the blanket from his wife holding the apple, he felt as if everything he'd ever believed in was gone. "Theodore? What are we going to do?"

His pet name for her. *Theodore.* Always when he said it, she poked fun at him and giggled and said, "Joe, this isn't Alvin and the Chipmunks."

But not today. Today she said, "We're going to do what the doctors tell us to do, I guess." A big breath in. "Either a lumpectomy or a mastectomy. And if the pathology report shows what they think it'll show, chemo and radiation after that." She took another bite of her sandwich. Joe tossed the apple into the basket, picked a piece of grass and threaded it between his two thumbs. When he blew to make it whistle, nothing happened.

"Of course, this is your chance, Joe. If you ever wanted a different woman . . ." He looked up, horrified, before he realized what she meant. "I could get big boobs," she went on, looking mischievous. "Have them remade to any size and specification. And I could change my hair. I could get a brunette wig. Or even go platinum. No more of this boring dishwater blonde. We could put me back together exactly the way you want me to be."

"I don't want you any other way except the way that you are right now."

She put the sandwich down and reached for his hand. "Well." Her eyes measured his with great care. "That's one choice that you *don't* have."

"You know what I mean. I was meaning it the nice way. That I wouldn't change anything if I didn't have to."

"I know what you meant," she said. "I do."

A Saran wrapper scudded away in the breeze. Neither of them made a move to capture it. "We're going to have to tell the girls. And your father." Joe looked away, then back at her face.

"I don't think I can tell my dad, Joe. After everything that happened with Mother, this is going to be harder on him than on anybody else."

"Not quite, but I hear you. We do have to say something to him soon, though, Theia."

She started to pack picnic items back into the basket. The jar of pickles. The untouched brownies. "Maybe you could be the one to talk to him. You're so good at saying the right things to people."

"Not about this." For all the things he might be afraid of, he feared this worse than he feared the cancer or even losing her. He felt like he was losing his faith. "I tell them to pray. I tell them to expect miracles. I say they can trust their Father in heaven. But maybe I've just been giving everyone the standard religious lingo all these years. Maybe I'm realizing it isn't so easy when you're talking about your own life." He could hardly hear his own voice by the time the sentence was finished.

"Others need you for a pastor, Joe. I need you for a husband."

He stopped her when she reached for the mustard bottle. "We're going to get through this, Theia."

In the leaves of the tall cottonwood trees around them, they could hear the wind rustling toward them before it arrived. She put the mustard into the basket with slow precision in spite of his hand on her arm. "I know we will," she said. "What other choice do we have?"

Telling

The best way to tell the girls, they decided, was to take them someplace they liked, to spend one special family day together, before breaking the news. They signed the girls out of school on a Tuesday, the day before Theia's surgery, and drove to Idaho Falls for a spree at the mall.

As they traveled the countryside, Theia watched leaves rattle across the road in front of the car. Fields had ripened and combines waited, parked atop the rolling hills like medieval guards silhouetted against the sky.

After an hour or so, the farmland gave way to subdivisions. City traffic began to pass them at speeds that made Theia dizzy.

"Can we go to the pet store first?" Heidi's voice asked from the back seat and the game of Hang Man she and Kate were playing.

"I want to go to the bookstore first." Theia glanced back as Kate drew an arm on Heidi's hanging body.

"Not sure where we'll stop first." Joe was readjusting the rearview mirror so he could see them. "We're going to have to take turns."

But once they'd gotten to Grand Teton Mall, the girls as usual were anxious to go their own ways. "*Please.* I'll meet you at the pet store in fifteen minutes," Kate pleaded. "All I want to do is look at the new book releases."

Heidi was pulling them in the opposite direction. "There's ferrets in the window. They're so cute. Can we go in and look at them?"

"We aren't getting a ferret, Heidi." Joe's voice was calm but firm.

"I know. But that doesn't mean I can't hold one." She disappeared into Pet City.

So much for family togetherness. "Maybe we shouldn't have done it this way, Joe," Theia said. "Maybe we've ruined one of their favorite things for them. Every time they come shopping from now on, they'll remember today."

"There isn't any 'best way' to do this." Joe circled an arm around her shoulders. "Anyway we do it, it's going to be—well, awful."

After everyone had spent time in the shops of their choice, they ate lunch at Garcia's. The four of them piled into a half-moon booth with paper flowers in jugs behind them and a bright piñata dangling overhead. The waitress served a basket of chips, bowls of salsa, and brought them all Dr. Peppers.

Joe took Theia's hand. "We brought you here because your mother and I needed a good place to talk to you."

Chips paused in midair. "What?" Four round eyes held identical expressions, a mix of curiosity and bewilderment.

Theia had practiced the words for so many days, but her voice seemed caught in her throat now. *What do I say? How do I tell them?* She forced the words from her mouth. "I'm going into the hospital tomorrow for some surgery."

Kate dipped her chip and munched it with feigned nonchalance. "What kind of surgery?"

"I won't be in there very long. Just two or three days, if everything goes well."

Heidi was peeling the paper meticulously off her straw, then left it lying beside her glass. "Can we come visit you?"

"I'd like that very much. And afterward, after I get home, I'll need to have some treatments. There's going to be plenty of times when I'll need you both to help me."

"Treatments for what, Mom?" Kate laid a chip on her plate and stared at her mother. "What do you have?"

Theia glanced at Joe, willing strength into all of them. "I have breast cancer."

Silence engulfed the table. The waitress came and placed hot plates in front of them. No one picked up a utensil. No one said a word. Until Heidi said what they were all thinking, with a hint of a cry in her voice. "But, Mama, some people die from breast cancer."

"Yes, I know that. But others don't."

"You're not going to die, are you?"

"I don't know, Heidi. No one knows for sure."

How could she attempt to reassure them, having no idea herself what lay ahead?

"Well, I know what's going to happen," Heidi said with sudden aplomb. "Nothing's going to happen to you. It can't. Jesus heals people who are sick."

"Sometimes."

"When they believe enough, he does. Like happened to everybody in the Bible."

"I don't know. Sometimes he lets other things happen, too. Even when people believe enough. We just have to trust that—that he's doing the right thing."

Lip service, all of it. When it came to trusting God right now, Theia knew that neither she nor Joe stood a chance. Ever since her diagnosis, she'd awakened every night, doubts assailing her, loneliness cutting into her, fear calling out to her from the dark corners of her bedroom.

A scripture came to her from out of nowhere. 'He who doubts is like a wave of the sea, blown and tossed by the wind. He is a double-minded man, unstable in all he does.'

They didn't discuss cancer again during the meal. What began as a festive occasion had degenerated to a hushed clinking of forks. When they walked back to the mall one last time, they stood and gazed in the window of Claire's Boutique while Kate went in with her own money to buy a birthday gift for Jaycee.

"Look at those over there." Theia pointed to a rack of blue satin headbands hanging on the wall. "See that fabric? I used to have hair ribbons made out of exactly the same pattern."

"You used to wear hair ribbons?" Joe zipped up his coat and rummaged in the pockets for his keys. "For some reason, I have a hard time picturing you in ribbons."

"I wonder where those went. I haven't seen them in years."

Heidi zipped up her coat too. She obviously wasn't interested in ribbons. "Does Grandpa Harkin know you've got cancer?"

"No, he doesn't yet. Everything was so hard for him when Mother died. I haven't figured out a way I can tell him about me."

"Mama, I'm scared about this."

Theia took Heidi in her arms, held her tight against her chest, so tight neither of them could breathe, so tight that their hearts seemed to clatter against one another. "You shouldn't be afraid, Heidi," she tried. But she wasn't very good at lying. "There really isn't anything to be scared of."

. . . .

Theia and her family entered the hospital through the wide panel of glass doors. A young mother was being wheeled out, her arms full of flowers and new baby. Theia turned her head to watch the little drama of a new family beginning a whole new chapter of their lives.

Once she'd gotten to the surgery center, she was led to a little room to change into the regulation uniform for operations. She carefully folded her clothes, one piece at a time, into the white plastic bag printed with bold blue letters, "Property of _____." *Does anyone ever take the time to actually write a name on one of those?*

She donned the threadbare gown, an equally threadbare wrap, thick socks, a paper cap. The girls and Joe each gave her a hug, a whispered "I love you," and waved good-bye. Then the gurney took Theia down one hall, up another, through double doors, as she wondered at the bright lights above her, the round mirrored balls at every corner, the pulsing colors.

When she opened her eyes, she felt as if hours had passed, as if all of life had gone by while she'd slept. Voices surrounded her, voices she didn't know. "There we go. We've got her. That's good."

A blood-pressure cuff tightened, released, tightened, released on her arm. Theia wanted it off. If she could scramble around and find it, she'd throw the thing across the room.

She needed to wake up, and she knew it. The girls and Joe were waiting for her. Heidi would be so tired of sitting around. She'd have at least ten get-well cards cut out and glued together by now. And Kate would be wandering the halls, begging another soda off Joe, dealing with this on teenager terms, silently, not talking until things were better, when she didn't have to show that she was afraid.

All at once, Theia knew she was going to be sick. Someone stood beside her head, holding back her hair, while she threw up into a towel.

"I'm sorry," she whimpered to everyone she didn't know. "I'm really sorry."

She didn't cry until she saw Joe. They'd led him into the recovery room, and here he came, looking handsome, his hands covering hers, the rhythm of the heart monitor beeping overhead, the IV threaded into her arm, oxygen tubes jabbing her nose.

"Hey, Theodore." How she loved the sound of his voice. "They're having a hard time bringing you around, I hear." He held her head and stroked her hair.

There were so many things she wanted to tell him. "Joe—"

"Sh-hhh. Don't talk now. Just rest."

She tried to raise her head. It flopped back of its own accord. "Are the girls tired of waiting for me?"

"The girls are in your room. They've got it all set up and ready. Heidi's got plenty of pictures drawn. And Kate's watching some game show."

"Tell them I love them."

"I will."

For long moments, she closed her eyes, slipping in and out of awareness. Her hand, taped and tethered with IV tubes, began roving. She searched for the bandages by feel; when she found them, she touched her bosom.

"Did they have to take all of it? Or did they leave a little bit?"

No matter how woozy the drugs still made her, Theia could already see the answer in his eyes. He'd been dreading this moment. Perhaps, like she'd done yesterday, he'd been practicing in his head, over and over again, what he should say.

"They had to take everything, Theia."

"It's gone? All of it?"

He nodded. "There was a lymph node involved. Dr. Waterhouse did what he had to do."

Fresh tears came and rolled down the sides of her face.

"I know, honey. I'm sorry." He kept stroking her hair. "It's going to be okay." They both realized, as he repeated himself for what seemed like the hundredth time, that the words were feeble and empty. "We're going to get through this."

"It isn't fair that my father has to do this twice."

"It was different with your mother, Theia. Everything has changed so much since then."

"No, not everything. So many things are still the same."

A tube led from her underarm, draining fluid into a bottle pinned to her hospital gown. She watched as it filled with peach-colored liquid. Everything ached. Keeping her eyes open, even. From behind them, an unnamed nurse began to work. One by one, she disconnected various wires and tubes. "We're taking you to your room now, Mrs. McKinnis." She hooked the IV bag to a rack where it could ride shotgun on the gurney. "They keep delivering flowers and balloons with your name on them. It's like a birthday down there."

The girls must have been watching for them and met them halfway down the hall, both of them exuberant and happy. "That took forever, Mom."

"Mrs. Clark and Mrs. Ballinger came by and sat with us for a little while."

"Everybody from the church is taking food over to the house. Only we told Rhonda Stuart not to make chicken tetrazzini because Dad hates mushrooms."

"Do you feel better, Mom?"

"No, silly. She feels worse. She just had her operation."

"Like the game. OPERATION! Did they take out your funny bone, Mom? I always make the buzzer go off."

The girls think it's over, don't they? They think I'm safe.

"No." Joe knotted his knuckle on Heidi's head. "I told the doctors to leave Mom's funny bone in."

"Very f-funny."

"Is the cancer gone? Did they get it out, Mom?"

Theia reached for Joe's hand, but he wasn't standing close enough for her to grasp it. But he answered for her. "We don't know the answer to that yet. We won't know if the doctors got all the cancer out for a very long time."

Harry Harkin plunged his spade deep into the soil, freeing the root-bound English ivy from its terra-cotta confines. He shook the roots free of old dirt, gingerly checking to make certain that the plant didn't have rot or nematodes, before he settled it with care into the soft new loam of a larger pot.

It always made him feel like praying, fiddling in the dirt. *Nothing like repotting plants to make one think about the Father*, he thought, humming as he tamped down new soil around the ivy stems. *Ever so often, a man gets root-bound. God has to pick him up and shake the soil out of his innards and transplant him to a larger pot.*

Usually, he'd been thankful for the transplant.

Sometimes, he hadn't been.

Harry rattled through his array of tubs and tins that fit together like the nesting soldiers he'd once played with as a boy. He glanced up and, through the wavy greenhouse glass in the fading light, saw his son-in-law drive into the driveway and his two granddaughters climb out.

Where had everybody been all day? Place had been way too quiet with the whole brood away.

Harry figured he had the best of both worlds, living in the father-in-law apartment the church elders had added onto the parsonage, being close to the grandkids, having his separate life and his life with his family, as well. More often than not, he knew the entire McKinnis clan's daily schedules and procedures. But for the past few weeks, everyone had been racing around so fast he'd lost track. Dance rehearsals. Girl Scout meetings. Swim team competitions. What have you. Enough to make an old man's head spin.

Now that he'd finished transplanting the ivy, he'd move on to other things. The church bazaar would come faster than he knew it, and everyone expected his annual offering of forced paper whites, just in time for the holidays. He'd just pulled out a burlap bag full of bulbs, sprouts already burgeoning from beneath oniony skin, when a knock sounded on the greenhouse screen door.

He walked over and opened it himself, a stack of planters in his hand. "Come in, come in," he said to Joe. Something in his son-in-law's face made him wary. "It's about time we ran into each other somewhere."

"I'm sorry, Dad. I've got—well, I have some difficult news to tell you."

There had been some discussion among the woman at the bazaar last year that he ought to root his paper whites in pebbles and not in dirt. He made his final decision just this minute and chose the dirt. He turned on the garden spigot and ran water. "Out with it then, son. No need to drag it out longer than you need to."

"Theia has breast cancer. She's had a mastectomy today."

Harry's hands faltered as they moved in the soil and the tepid water. "Today?"

As the truth began to rage inside him, he wasn't certain what made him angrier. That Theia had cancer, or that they'd waited until after the surgery to tell him.

"Come help me mix this, Joe. Make yourself useful." They stood side-by-side, old man and younger one, making mud pies. *Please, Father,* he finally got himself calm enough to pray. *Not my daughter too.*

"You might have told me a little sooner than this, Joe," he said, holding his tone as matter of fact as he could. "I could have been at the hospital today."

"We didn't want you to be worrying unnecessarily."

Harry looked at his son-in-law. "I wouldn't have been worrying. I would have been praying."

"You know why we waited, Dad. It's because of everything that happened to Edna. Theia thought this would be harder on you than on anybody else. I don't think she could have gotten through it today, knowing that you were upset." Joe's voice kind of ran down at the end.

Harry said it again, for emphasis. "I would have been *praying*, not worrying." But maybe Theia was right. Maybe he wouldn't have. After what had happened to his wife, he ought to be terrified, thinking such a sickness would come after his daughter too. Didn't they say that your chances of having cancer were higher if it ran in your family?

He turned from Joe and fiddled with the burlap bag. He handed three bulbs from the sack to Joe, each of them plump and succulent. "You plant these. It's nice when they've got tops on them like this. That way you know which end is up."

Do you want me to trust you with this, Lord? Do I trust you, or do I trust that medicine is different now?

Or do I just trust that you wouldn't take two women away from the same old man?

He had to hand it to Joe. He looked a whole lot more comfortable standing behind a pulpit than he did planting bulbs into buckets. But Joe did as he had been told, burying the paper whites deep and then sprinkling them with Harry's massive watering can. For long moments, they stood silent except for the *glub glub glub* of moisture sinking into the soil, the pleasantly natural sound of something drinking.

You moving me from one pot to a bigger one, Lord? You out to show me something about my roots? Have I been sinking them too deep in the wrong places?

It then occurred to him that the man who stood beside him had every bit as strong a reason to feel mad and lost. He turned. Paying no heed to his dirt-encrusted fingers, he wrapped his arms around the man whose marriage had made him a son. "You're working mighty hard to hold back your sorrow, aren't you, Joe?"

Joe hugged him back, hard. Harry felt Joe's warm breath against his ear. "You're right. I don't know what to do now, Dad. I don't know what to say to people. I don't know what to believe." Joe's voice broke even though it was only a whisper.

Harry let the tears come, and he could feel dampness on his shoulder from Joe.

They stood there awhile in the greenhouse, taking solace from the fact that they had held onto each other and maybe felt better for it.

Father, help me to lay down everything I'm afraid of and minister to this man who needs me. Needs you. Lord Jesus, you're going to have to bring about something good from this, because I sure as heck can't see it's going to come from anyplace else.

"You've got me, Joe. There's not much good about me, other than the fact that I've already been through this once. Maybe the good Lord can make some use of that."

Joe gave him a hug and stepped back, pulling a handkerchief from his pocket. "I've got to go put supper on the table for the girls. Theia has things ready in the freezer. . . ." But he didn't finish the sentence and turned toward the door. "Want to join us, Dad?" he said over his shoulder.

Harry shook his head. "Not tonight. Thanks. And say hi to the girls for me." He watched his son-in-law, head low, cross the lawn.

Where Are You, Lord?

This week Joe had canceled at least five counseling appointments at his church office.

He had neither the time nor the inclination to listen to other people's problems.

"Perception," he always told everyone during the sessions. It's a matter of perception. When you see something as being hopeless, it will be.

He leaned back in his office chair and stared out the window at the church lawn. He'd left the hospital this afternoon because he simply couldn't bear to be near the antiseptic smell any longer, wandering around the halls of St. John's like someone lost, thanking people for bringing flowers and food, feeling useless . . . hopeless.

He'd been moved by his father-in-law's response to the news. Where Harry might have railed at the injustice of Theia's cancer, he'd responded to Joe's pain instead.

Is that what you do, Lord? Use men who have been broken and emptied to minister, so everyone will know that it's you?

It occurred to him that this was the first time since they'd diagnosed his wife that he'd spoken directly to God.

He'd gotten so tired of putting on the charade.

She needs you to be strong for her, and you're nothing but a fraud. He didn't know if that was God talking to him, or his own demons, or . . .

His secretary, Sarah Hodges, buzzed on his intercom. "Joe? The church decorating committee is here. They're meeting in the adult Sunday school room. They're asking if you can join them."

He'd procrastinated with church business for as long as he could. He'd already instructed Sarah to keep all his appointments on the books today. "Tell them I'll be there in a few minutes." He moved over to the window, took a deep breath, and started for the door. Maybe decorating was the most he was up for.

When he walked in the room, he knew very soon he was in the middle of an ongoing debate, and these women, faithful volunteers all, were looking for an umpire to call the plays.

"I think it's a shame we don't put a tree at the front of the church," announced Mary Cathcart. "We used to do that when we were in the small sanctuary, and it was beautiful."

"I don't like the idea of a tree beside the altar. It puts too much emphasis on secular Christmas celebrations."

"We made Christian decorations for it one year. Cut them out of those white trays they use for the meat at Albertson's and outlined them with glitter. Mangers, fish, and crosses."

"People like getting married that time of year because they can have the tree."

"I think we ought to put the manger scene on the chancel. That's what we need to emphasize."

"We need to have a Saturday potluck where everyone comes prepared to decorate. A church-wide hanging-of-the-greens ceremony."

"The Presbyterians always do a hanging-of-the-greens. They'll think we're copying them."

"Well, aren't we?"

They quieted down and turned as one to stare at Joe.

"We shouldn't copy the Presbyterians," was all he could think to say. When he finally slipped away with a meaningful look at his watch, the discussion was continuing in a more open dialogue.

Next on Joe's agenda came a meeting with his choir director, Ray Johnson.

"The youth worship team feels the Lord is leading them to do a song this Sunday called 'Love To The Highest Power.'"

"It sounds like a song with a good message."

"It's rock, Joe. I think it might scare some people."

Joe scrubbed his forehead with his fingers. "Can you convince them to wait a week or two? We'll call it youth Sunday or something. That way nobody will be offended."

After Ray left, Joe smoothed the wrinkles in his shirt, puffed up his cheeks so the air went out of him like a balloon.

When Dr. Waterhouse had come to the room to see Theia early this morning, he'd told them everything they didn't want to hear. "Your tumor did not have a distinct boundary, Mrs. McKinnis. We are reasonably certain that we got it all. Not positive, but reasonably certain."

"When can you be more than reasonably certain? When can we be positive?" Joe couldn't help voicing his questions.

"After her treatments are over, if there are no new recurrences in five years. Then we can be positive."

"Five years? She's going to have to live with this—this uncertainty for five years?"

The surgeon was making notes on his clipboard. "We hope so, Mr. McKinnis."

His last appointment of the day, and he'd been dreading it the most. He walked into the front office, held out his hand to Winston

Taylor for a handshake. The man owned a construction company, and his rather loud, hearty personality wasn't exactly one to which Joe naturally gravitated. He already knew the subject they'd be discussing. He'd been counseling with Winston for a year about a personal issue that had broken his relationship with the Lord. Had there been any progress? They seemed to cover the same ground too often.

"Thanks for making time for me, Joe." Winston toted his Bible with him, tucked beneath one elbow of his sheepskin coat.

"Come on back, Win." *Lord, help me . . .* something he often prayed before these encounters with Winston Taylor.

The man shut the door behind him, and they were alone. Joe settled the man in one of the overstuffed chairs arranged in a conversational grouping, settling himself in the chair opposite. He crossed his legs, cleared his throat, waited for the other man to begin.

"You're going to be surprised at what I came here to talk about." Winston uncrossed his own legs and leaned forward. "I came here to talk about you and your wife."

"Theia and I are fine, Winston. There's no need worrying about that."

"That's not what the Lord's been telling me, Pastor Joe. Every time I start out trying to pray for something else, *bam*! There I am praying for you two instead. Seems to me there must be a battle going on. And it isn't about what's going on in her body. It's about what's going on in your heart."

Joe gave a strangled chuckle. It was the only way he knew to cover the tears welling in his own eyes, the grief welling in his spirit. "I thought I was supposed to be the pastor here," he finally managed to get out without sounding like a basket case.

"As I see it, Joe McKinnis, the Lord wants something specific from you right now. He wants you to shut down all the trappings of being religious, and he wants you to figure out what it is from him that you're expecting."

"Expecting? I don't know what you mean." Joe also leaned forward, elbows braced on his knees, hands steepled.

"How do you think everybody felt when the soldiers crucified Jesus? How do you think they felt when Jesus died?"

"I guess I don't see what that has to do with—with this situation."

"It has *everything* to do with it."

"How so?"

"Stop for a minute and think what Christ's followers *expected* on his crucifixion day. Then think about what they *got*. In the end, a thousand fold more. But Christ had to *die* as they stood there waiting for miracles to happen."

Joe felt like he had been stabbed in the heart with that last emphasized word. But slowly he felt himself begin to nod. "I understand that part of it. The grief, the pain, the fear—all the feelings they had were warranted."

"Those folks had to go through the experience from top to bottom. They experienced all the anguish and then all the restoration. If they had to put names on things, what would they have asked for? For it never to have happened? For Christ to have walked away free? There was a small group—a *very* small group—that expected Jesus to conquer the grave. And at the same time, don't you know that they were afraid to expect that very thing?"

"Perhaps." A glimmer of truth began to flicker into life in Joe's heart.

"Then there were the ones who never expected anything at all. The moment Christ gave up the ghost on the cross, life was over as they knew it. Nothing looked the way they'd expected it to look. Nobody dared to hope. Then the impossible happened. An empty tomb. Mary Magdalene in the garden. All of them so sure he was gone that when they saw him walking they didn't even *recognize* him."

Joe stared at the floor between his legs. He shook his head slowly. "I don't know, Win. I'm just not sure."

"Neither were they, Joe." Winston Taylor closed his Bible with a slap, tucked it beneath his armpit, and reached over to put his hand on Joe's shoulder. "I can tell you one thing, Joe. What's going to happen is going to happen, whether you are expecting it or not. But what you *expect* from Theia's situation is going to directly influence the way you *see* it."

Winston stood and took his leave, and Joe went back to his desk. He picked up a picture of his family and stared at Theia's pretty, hopeful face.

She'd given away parts of her own life so she could be his wife. Her degree at University of Colorado. Her chance to be a dancer, to either perform or to teach, to make a difference in students' lives. All this, but she'd married him instead, had settled in to become a minister's wife. She'd fed him and nurtured him through seminary, home-schooled the girls, cleaned and cooked, put up with 3 a.m. phone calls, modest salary, dickering, disciplining.

What do I expect, Lord?

This hurt so much. If only he, instead of his wife, could be battling cancer. Maybe he was fooling himself, but he didn't think so. It would be so much easier if it had been him.

Do I expect peace? Assurance that you will heal her? That she could go through all of this and not have to be afraid?

He buried his face in his hands.

Expect Me, Beloved.

But he didn't hear it. Joe's hot tears overpowered everything else, the phone's ringing in the office, the Mothers of Preschoolers meeting in the Fellowship Hall, the insistent, gentle voice calling, calling, giving him the very answer he sought.

"It's okay, Grandpa." Theia heard outside her hospital room. "If Mom's sleeping, we can wake her up. She wants to see you."

Theia rolled her head sideways on the pillow. "Hey, you." She shot Kate a little sad smile as her daughter's face appeared around the doorframe. "What's up?"

"Just checking on you. Grandpa's been driving me all around town in his old car."

Theia pushed herself against the mattress and did her best to sit higher. She winced. "Hi, Daddy."

Harry came to the foot of the bed, a pot of pink geraniums in his hand. "Since Joe came to tell me what was going on, thought I'd better stop on over for a visit."

"Those are beautiful."

"They ought to be, coming from my greenhouse."

Kate took the flowers from him and set them, exuberant in their lacy brightness, in the window ledge.

"Thought getting that old Ford Fairlane out of the meadow would be a good excuse." Now that he'd gotten rid of the flowers, he doffed his tweed hat. He kept turning his hat, turning his hat, his gnarled fingers clenching the woolen cloth. "Thought I'd best come over here and let you know that I know."

She could guess at everything he wanted to say to her, every simple reassurance he wanted to offer her. But if he gave them, he'd be wrong. "I'm so sorry, Daddy."

Joe might have said, "I never wanted this to happen to you, Dad."

Theia might have said, "I never wanted you to go through this all over again, with someone else you loved."

But neither of them would delve into the past—or the future— in front of Kate.

So they talked about the Ford instead. "I can't believe you got that old car started. And with the weather this cold, too."

"Had to drive down to Shervin's and get a new battery for it first. Once she turned over, though, that was it. She's purred like a kitten ever since."

Kate piped in with, "Grandpa says I can have it when I start driving, Mom. He thinks it'll be the perfect car for a teenager."

It was clear Harry hadn't wanted Kate to announce it like that. He appeared a little sheepish. "Thought that might take everybody's mind off other things."

Theia's lunch came rattling in on a metal cart. The candy striper moved a basket of daisies, a box of tissues, and situated the tray on the rolling table.

"You want something to eat, Kate? You can get a hamburger in the cafeteria. There's money in my bag."

"I've got money." Harry plopped his hat on Theia's feet and fished out his wallet. He unfolded his money and counted out three dollar bills.

He was getting so slow. If Theia hadn't been sick, she'd have taken the bills from her purse and whisked Kate out the door before he'd even had the chance to pitch in. Those hands. Hands that had held her as a baby. She hadn't noticed they were growing so feeble.

Let Daddy live for a long time, Lord. I don't want to have to do without him.

Reality came back to her with a jolt.

I have cancer.

What right did she have to wish for a long life for her father when she might not even be around to spend it with him?

"Thanks, Grandpa." Kate took the proffered bills. "I'll probably just get a soda anyway. You want me to bring you anything?"

He shook his head. "I ate at home."

Kate headed out the door and, the moment she did, the mood between Theia and her father changed. Harry seemed, in that instant, to sag. He lowered himself with stiff arms into the plastic chair as if his entire being had begun to ache. "Joe came over and told me everything last night."

"Of all the people who needed to know, I hated for you to hear this news."

"You'd better eat your lunch. It's going to get cold."

"Jell-O is already cold. I won't do much harm to it by waiting."

"You need to do everything the doctors tell you to do."

"I will. I promise, Daddy."

"You get plenty of rest. You've got to do everything they know to do to fight this thing."

"I'm thinking it will be different for me, Daddy. They found my lump so much earlier than they found Mama's. And treatments now are much more advanced."

"You take care of yourself. And take care of Joe. I told him last night, I may not be good for much, but I've been through this once. Maybe I can steer him in the right direction some."

"He needs that. Everybody depends on him so."

Harry fiddled with the window blinds and peered out. "Remember those nights when you were a little girl, when you called me every night to come check underneath your bed?"

It seemed forever ago, Theia's little-girl life. The heavy sound of her father's footsteps in the hall when he would lock up the house before bed. The way the mattress sank when he'd sit beside her in the dark.

"I was just thinking the other day about those old hair ribbons passed down from Grandma Stewart. Remember? Mama would tie them in my hair and tell me they'd keep me from being afraid."

"We used to be so frustrated, Edna and I. You went through about a year of your life when it took you hours to go to sleep. We'd be waiting in the bedroom, thinking we'd never get any time alone together. You know . . . to be, well, romantic."

"Daddy!"

"That's what we'd do."

She gazed at her father with all of her love for him pouring forth from her heart. "Thank you for all those nights, Daddy. For all those times when you told me there wasn't anything to be afraid of."

"If only I could tell you the same thing now . . ."

Coming to Terms

When the phone began ringing, Heidi raced through the kitchen, slipping on the linoleum in her socks, doing her best to beat her sister.

"I don't know why you're in such a hurry to answer the phone." Kate perched beside the sink, nonchalantly crisscrossing a new Delia's ribbon shoelace into her sneakers. "It's just somebody else calling to see if Mom got home from the hospital okay. Or it might be for me."

This same scenario had been playing out in the McKinnis household for months. Two sisters, each vying for calls. "But it just might be for me." Heidi rounded the kitchen counter and grabbed the receiver.

"It isn't for you. It's never for you. If it isn't about Mom, it's for me. Everyone wants to talk about the car Grandpa Harkin's giving me."

"Hello?" Heidi almost couldn't speak for panting. "McKinnis residence."

"I'd like to speak with Heidi McKinnis, please."

Heidi poked out her chin and grinned at her sister in a blatant gesture of victory. "This is Heidi."

"This is Julie Stevens from Dancers' Workshop. Do you have a minute? There's something I'd like to talk to you about."

"I have a minute." At the sound of such astonishment in Heidi's voice, even Kate stopped to listen.

"Good." A hesitation. "Well, you see, it's this. I'm making a change or two in the *Nutcracker* performance."

"Oh, I'm so sorry I missed practice last Saturday. My mom was in the hospital. I promise I'll be there next week."

"I know all about that. Missing practice every once in a while is nothing to be concerned about. But I do want to talk to you about your role as an angel."

"You do? Okay . . ."

"As you know, Heidi, the angels are an audience favorite each year. Gauzy wings, hoop skirts, the tiniest floating steps, the youngest most angelic girls we can find."

"My mom tells me that every year."

"I hope you don't mind that I'm needing to change things."

"Change things?" Heidi gripped the receiver. "What do you mean?"

"I'd like to change your part, Heidi, if you don't mind."

"I don't mind."

"I'm having trouble with the clowns this year. I didn't cast as many for some reason and, for the choreography to come off the way I want it to, I've got to bring in another girl."

"Yes?" Heidi held her breath.

"Do you think you might be interested?"

"I'm interested, all right. I love the clowns. That's always been my favorite part, seeing everyone come out from under Mother Ginger's skirt."

"Of course, this doesn't give you as long to learn the part as the others. They've already been dancing it for six weeks. But I'll bet you can pull it off."

"I can. I know I can."

"As part of the choreography, you'll have to turn a cartwheel. Do you know how to turn a cartwheel?"

Heidi faltered. "No. I—I don't."

"Do you think you could learn? Is there someone who can teach you?"

"My mother can show me how."

"That's it, then. We're all set. Rehearsal time is the same. Only you'll be dancing in studio three instead of studio one."

"I'll be there. I promise I'll be there."

"Someone will measure you Saturday so we can fit you with a costume."

"Thank you. I'll be a good clown. You'll see."

"Perfect. We'll see you on Saturday."

On Sunday before church, it snowed.

A brisk tinge in the air came first, and then the flakes, small just as the sun rose, then larger, a confetti celebration outside the windows.

Snow blanketed the grass and etched a scalloped edge along the picket fence. At the morning service, excitement from outside carried into the sanctuary. A vast jumble of coats, from ski parkas to even a few furs, hung on pegs in the front vestibule. Snow boots lay in disarray, no two together the same. Folks shivered and laughed and tucked their gloves away, talking about the mountain, when the runs would open for skiing, if the new snow had brought elk down into the refuge out of the hills.

Theia moved into the front pew with her husband, the place they always sat, their two daughters flanking them. Harry joined them sometimes when he didn't opt to sit with his friends.

She couldn't think about the church service at hand. She couldn't think about the fresh snow outside. She could only think about breast cancer. Her mind drifted. Worried. Wondered. Wandered.

Had the cancer spread to other parts of her body?

If it hadn't yet, would it, still?

And then . . . ?

As music began to fill the sanctuary, Kate and Jaycee sidled into places beside them.

"Where's your sister?"

"Oh, she'll get here. She's probably back in the Sunday school room helping the little kids clean up."

"She's probably back in the Sunday school room trying to get extra Hershey Bars from Mrs. Taggart." Jaycee was so much part of the family she even teased like them.

One by one, the women sitting in the row behind Theia began to tap her on the shoulder or nod their heads at her or wish her well. We were worried about you. We've been praying. Are you okay? Is there anything we can do to help? We know how you must feel.

She gave the same response, the same answers to each of them. Thank you for praying. No need to worry. Everything's fine. You know how it is.

Lord, please. I don't want to be here. I shouldn't have come to church today. It's too soon. I'm not ready for this.

Theia felt as if she was drowning in the deep, flailing about, exhausted, trying to keep her head up where she could breathe.

Why did they all have to be so sympathetic? Why couldn't they talk about something else? Why couldn't they share their own problems, or something fun that was going on?

Why couldn't they pretend that none of this was happening?

Theia glanced down to see a little boy she'd taught in Vacation Bible School at her knees. He threw his arms around her legs and hugged her. He gazed up at her with dark eyes so wide and pure, she wanted to cry out.

"Hello, Landon." Despite the missing oblique muscle, the tight tendons, she managed to lift him cautiously into her arms. It felt so odd, hugging him this way. Just holding a small child's body against her wounded chest brought a new sense of loss that overwhelmed her. She ached to be whole again. The little boy planted a wet kiss on her cheek. "I love you," he whispered.

"I love you, too, Landon." She couldn't keep the tears back.

Lord, I'm the pastor's wife. I can't tell anybody that I'm afraid. I have no right to.

Everyone around her kept offering advice. You ought to meet Joe Beth Mason. She's a cancer survivor. She's doing really well. I have a miracle book you can read. All about the herbal things you can do. We know you can do this, Theia, said with a careful I-know-you-can-do-it smile.

Landon's mother came to take him away, and when the next person tapped her on the shoulder, she turned, expecting another embrace.

Instead she found herself face-to-face with Sue Masterson.

Mrs. Masterson did not reach out in love and offer pleasantries. She pointed out the front window and jabbed her finger as she enunciated each word. "Do you have any idea what your daughter is doing?"

She'd forgotten all about Heidi. Theia glanced about, hoping to find her daughter standing with some friend in the service. But

Heidi wasn't in the sanctuary. And Mrs. Taggart, her Sunday school teacher, had already come into the room and situated herself with her family. Theia gave a half-guilty shrug. "Well, no. I guess I don't."

"You'd better go find out." Sue planted her hands on her hips and gave a righteous toss of her head. "She's outside in the parking lot terrorizing little children with snowballs."

"Oh, that's ridiculous."

Theia knew this about herself. Above all else, she would fight for the honor of her family. She'd done the exact thing when she'd gone to speak with Julie Stevens about Heidi's dancing. "I'll bet those kids are all having fun in the snow."

In her velvet skirt. In the forty-dollar clogs I bought her from Broadway Toys-n-Togs.

"You ought to see what she's done to Dillon. He's drenched from head to toe. I'm embarrassed to bring him into the service. Water is running from his hair. He's out there *crying.*"

"He's crying? Because he got a little wet?"

"He's crying because your daughter shoveled snow down his pants."

Oh, dear. For the first time in weeks, Theia found something comical. She felt like doubled-over, stitches in her side, bellyache laughter. Glorious. Splendid.

But Sue Masterson had to go and spoil it all. "For heaven's sake, Theia. Your kids are the preacher's kids. They're supposed to act better than everyone else, aren't they?"

I can't do this, Lord. I cannot do this.

Without telling Joe where she was headed, she laid her Bible on the seat and ducked out. She hurried to the front vestibule to find her coat. There she found poor Dillon Masterson, his hair plastered flat to his head and a dark patch of wet spreading down to the knees of his cargo pants.

She tilted her head at Dillon. "You okay?"

He nodded.

"So Heidi did this to you?"

He nodded again.

She rumpled his wet hair with her one operable arm. At least *some* good had come of his snowball fight. His face was cleaner than she'd seen it in weeks. "You go on in there with your mother."

"But I'm wet."

"The Lord doesn't care if you're wet. Only mothers care about something like that." She gave him a little pat-shove in the proper direction.

Theia found a troupe of fifth graders outside, acting like they owned the world, bellowing and running and smearing each other with snowballs. She got there just in time to see Heidi get walloped in the head.

Heidi wasted no time retaliating. She scooped up snow, packed it hard between her hands, and let it fly. "Take that, you slime ball."

The sphere hit its target, Trey Martin's backside, and exploded into icy particles. "Heidi Louise McKinnis," Theia shouted. "You come here this instant."

Amazing how silence could fall on a group of fifth graders.

"Hi, Mom."

"You want to tell me what's going on out here?"

"Snowball fights. We're killing each other."

"Do you think this is the proper thing to be doing right now, out in the church parking lot calling your classmates 'slime ball' while there's a worship service going on inside?"

"But it's *snowing.*"

"I know, and if I were ten years old, I'd feel the same way. But, I'm not. I'm your mother. And Dillon Masterson is inside with a major problem."

"Am I in trouble?"

"That depends."

"On what?"

"Do you think you owe Dillon an apology?"

"No."

Theia stood in the snow, waiting, using the silent, stern approach, hoping her daughter would recant. But Heidi did no such thing.

"You won't apologize?"

"No."

"You'd better examine your heart, young lady."

"You should have heard what he said at school on Friday, Mom. He told Miss Vickers that the only reason I got moved up from angel to clown is because you've got cancer and everybody found out and they got worried if they didn't let me dance some other part this year that you'd never get to see it."

Theia felt like she'd been booted in the gut. The unexpected force of truth almost knocked her to her knees.

"I told him you were going to see me dance plenty. I told him he was stupid."

"Well, good for you. That's exactly what you needed to say."

"Dillon says I dance like a *chicken.*"

"That is a cruel thing to say." The words pushed Theia to the brink. Her words blazed with passion. "Listen to me. You are a beautiful dancer. A *wonderful* dancer. You dance like a princess." Oh, how she wanted to say more. She wanted to tell Heidi that she'd gotten the part because Julie Stevens must have noticed how she'd improved, or how she'd learned new steps, or how hard she'd tried. But she couldn't tell Heidi those things. Not a one of them. Because Dillon Masterson's words had struck their mark, wounded well. Theia cupped her daughter's cheeks inside her own two cold hands. "Do you hear me? Don't you ever let *anybody* tell you that you can't do something you want to do."

I can't do these things, Father. I can't tell her that Dillon's wrong. About her dancing he's wrong. But perhaps he isn't wrong about me. . . .

Heidi grinned, her face innocent and open. "Mom, I know you're going to get better. Jesus healed people in the Bible all the time."

"Let's go inside. Your father will be disappointed if we miss his sermon. You know how he always likes us to tell him that it was good."

"I'm not worried, Mom. I've been praying. Up in the tree house. It's quiet up there. God could hear me."

That's just what I told my own mother before she died. Jesus wouldn't let this happen. God has a big plan.

That's what she'd believed every day when she'd been young, every day while her mother had been sick, every day until her mother had died.

What Is Love, Anyway?

That night, Joe lay on his side of the big king-sized mattress, his lamp on, his pajama shirt rumpled, his big study book propped open against a cushion on his chest.

Theia lay on her side of the bed, blankets bunched up around her and caught between her legs. She kept her back toward him, her pillow plumped beneath her head as if she'd fallen asleep.

He knew from her breathing that she wasn't asleep at all.

Joe turned a page in his book, looked at it, turned back. He had no idea what he'd just read.

"You want me to go with you tomorrow?" he asked.

"Go with me where?"

"To chemo."

"There isn't any need for you to go. They say I won't feel bad until I've had several sessions. The effects are cumulative."

"I'd still like to be there."

She readjusted the pillow beneath her head and snuggled down deeper. "I don't want you to come, Joe."

"I want to be there for you, Theia. You told me that you didn't need me for a pastor, that you needed me for a husband. At least let me be that much for you."

"I was asleep. You woke me up."

"No, you weren't."

She sighed, didn't disagree with him.

"Was the sermon okay today?"

"It was good."

"I'm not so sure."

"It was."

"Frank Martin looked bored. And Sue Masterson couldn't stop drying off Dillon with Kleenex the entire time."

"Hmm."

He recognized her brusque, short sentences were his cue that she wanted quiet. He shut the book with a crack and laid it on his bedside table. Then he waited, watching, hoping his wife would turn to him. Only she didn't. His hand, the very extension of the depths of him that yearned to reach for her, felt leaden and heavy. Last night, he'd dreamed that he'd reached for her and hadn't found anything there.

"Theodore?"

"Hmm?"

"How long do we have to wait before"—he couldn't figure out exactly how to say it—"well, you know?" Perhaps he hadn't any right to want her, not now, not after everything she'd been through. But he had the sense that she'd cut herself off so completely from him, from everything around her, that it would be almost impossible to bring her back.

He heard her voice catch. "We don't have to wait if we don't want to."

But she didn't move toward him. She didn't move at all.

"Or we can wait."

"Yes."

Dear Father, I want to touch my wife. I don't care that her breast is gone. How do I show her that she is everything to me?

A good five minutes of silence passed. Outside the parsonage, a hay truck rattled past on the highway, carrying its two-ton limit, no doubt on its way to deliver a load to one of the local ranches. The lampshade rattled, and the truck's wheels rumbled up through the floor. Joe stared at the ceiling above them. Theia was still turned toward the wall on her side of the bed.

He tried to imagine what he would do, loving her the way he did, if he ever had to go through one day without her.

The weight of everything they carried together tonight felt like the truck outside, with its huge load of hay, running across their hearts, crushing them both.

"Theia." This time, Joe couldn't keep himself from reaching out to her. He turned back the covers and placed his hand on the slope of her shoulder, bunching her nightgown in a way that had always given him pleasure. The slightest bit of pressure now, and she would roll toward him, loop her arms around his neck.

"My—my breast isn't there anymore," she sobbed up at him, wrapping her forearms around the nape of his hair. "You shouldn't expect me to be beautiful anymore. I'm all—all cut away."

"No, Theia, not true. Everything I need is right here in my arms. None of that matters to me."

"It does matter. You'll have to help me change the dressing soon, and then you'll see it. It's horrible."

"But you are still *you* inside. You'll still be beautiful, Theia. I love your smile more than your breasts."

"There's an ugly trail of dots from the stitches. My body looks like someone tried to sew up the corners of a cushion."

"Don't you know? You're beautiful to me because I love you. Because of everything we've shared."

"This cancer has—has eaten a part of me away. It's eaten a part of my *faith* away."

"I think you're beautiful because I've watched you give birth to my babies."

"Why would God put me in the very same battle he gave my mother? A battle that we all had to sit and watch her lose?"

He'd stopped thinking clearly, perhaps. He was enjoying winning her over, saying all the right things. "I think you're beautiful because I know how goofy you acted when we were young. Because I was with you the time you stood up on the roller coaster at the fair. Because I know you're going to be all snaggle-toothed and funny looking when we both get old together."

It took Joe a full ten seconds to realize the terribly wrong thing he'd said. He froze. For a moment she just lay there, staring at him like she hadn't heard him right. Then her countenance crumpled in pieces. Her chin began to quiver. Her mouth contorted. Her eyes welled with tears.

"Theodore, I'm sorry. I'm so sorry."

She shoved him away, cast the rest of the blankets aside, and jumped out of bed. "How could you say that? *How could you say that?*"

"I didn't mean to. I wasn't thinking. I'm sorry."

She pulled on a sweatshirt over her nightgown.

"Where are you going, Theia?"

"I don't know. I'm just *going.*"

He was up, and beside her. "I'm coming, too."

"No you aren't. I want to be alone."

"It's the middle of the night. You can't go—."

"I'm a big girl, Joe." She hissed the words at him, no doubt to avoid waking the girls. But he was sure she would have screamed at him if they were alone in the house. "I go out walking at all times of day and night, *by myself.* Just because you've said something stupid doesn't give you the right to come along with me."

He couldn't stop himself. He'd borne the burden too long. "How can you act like this is just about you? If something happens to you, Theia, it happens to both of us. If you die"—he stood in the middle of the room, amid blankets scrambled on the floor in angry knots, his hands balled into incapable fists at his side—"If you die, everything for me ends too. You have to think about us in this together, not just you."

Beneath the sweatshirt and jacket, Theia's nightgown clung to her body damp with sweat. The hurt hammered with every heartbeat, a rhythmic throb of grief. Her teeth chattered. She pulled her coat tighter as she stumbled across the unbroken snow, her boots stamping waffle patterns behind her. When she looked over her shoulder, she could just make out the shape of the church and the parsonage and Harry's greenhouse, pink-washed in the moonlight.

She couldn't tell Joe, but nights had become excruciating for her. More often than not, she lay awake in the dark, held flat against the mattress by sorrow and fear and loneliness. The shadows pressed in on every side, became something alive, virulent. Chemo terrified her. Cancer petrified her.

"Father," she whispered aloud to the sky. "I'm not any good at this. I can't praise you. I can't pray. Your name is like dry sand in my mouth."

She couldn't bear the thought of standing in front of Joe with the ugly suture, the violated flesh, in view. She turned away from him in their bed, longing for what they had before, but dreading that first time when he would discover the awful disfigurement for himself.

Theia stared up at stars, pinpricks in the night sky. She listened, heard only unerring silence, only the rustle of breeze in the trees. She stood in the midst of the snowfield, her long shadow refracted in the moonlight, her own steps solitary behind her, and cried. "I can't do this, God. I can't be strong for everybody else. I can't even be strong for me."

So many things she needed. To be held close and rocked, to hear the affirmations that everyone around her could no longer give. To hold her children close and know that she would be alive to enjoy their growing.

"You've got so much food here," Laura Jones had said last week when she'd brought over lasagna. "You aren't going to have to cook for a *year*." Only trying to be lighthearted and friendly, but it was all so *lame*.

Theia cried now because Joe said she'd be beautiful when she was old. She didn't even know if she'd have the privilege of growing old. She cried now because Laura Jones had taken stock of her freezer.

Did it occur to anybody that she might *want* to cook? That she might hold dear a hundred different chores, because nothing guaranteed that she'd be around for those chores in another year?

I didn't want Joe to see me, to touch me. But that's one less time for him to touch me in the time that we have left.

"Nobody understands this, Lord," she cried aloud to the sky. "Nobody understands anything at all."

How she yearned for her father's arms. Not the feeble, aged way Harry held her lately, but the strong, big way he'd hugged her when she'd been a little girl. More tears. "I don't have the strength for this." Had she already said that? Unfathomable loneliness poured forth, overcame her. Her nose dripped. She did nothing to stop it. "I'm mad at you, God. Mad. MAD. How could you do this? How *could* you?"

She'd never been so afraid in all her life.

She'd never been so *angry*.

"Is this what you've planned, God? Is it?"

She struggled forward a few more steps in the snow. Then, as clearly as if she had lived it yesterday, Theia remembered her eighth birthday, standing in the backyard barefooted, the grass like lace beneath her toes. A truck from Preston Lumber turned into the alley, so big she thought it might knock down their neighbor's fence. And then a crane lifted her new playhouse, its wood fragrant and stark, into the corner beside the patio.

Harry had hugged her as Edna carried out boxes of doll furniture, hidden in her closet. "Happy Birthday, Theia."

"I've sewn you some curtains." Her mother handed her a box. "You want to hang them up?"

"She's going to have to wait fifteen minutes or so, Edna." Harry waggled a screwdriver in the air. "I don't have the curtain rods hung yet."

"Oh, Mama." She ran from one window to the other and peered in. "It's the prettiest house I've ever seen."

"Here's something else." Edna handed her a package wrapped in tissue. Theia unfolded the tissue. There in her hand lay a doll-sized embroidery framed in a hoop, carefully signed and dated by her mother. "Jesus Loves Me, This I Know." Her mother kissed her on the forehead. "This will make it feel like home."

That had been a long, long time ago.

No dolls anymore, but real daughters.

No tiny wooden furniture, but a living room of Thomasville instead.

Jesus Loves Me . . .

Do you? Do you really? Because, of you do, why would you take my mother away? Why would it happen to her, and then to me, too?

Dr. Sugden aligned the charts and the diagram flat on his desk for her to see. Class IIA cancer. Upper right quadrant of the right breast.

Not the sort of cancer that goes away without a fight, he said. The sort that, if you live, you live with. The sort of cancer that, if you survive, it makes you certain you are a survivor.

Where are you in this, Father? I can't find you, no matter how hard I try.

If he loved you, if he really cared about you, none of this would have happened. A God who loves his children wouldn't let anything like this come into your life.

I have drawn you with loving-kindness. I have loved you with an everlasting love.

That means he isn't there at all, don't you see? If he were there, you wouldn't feel like he wasn't. You shouldn't have this awful emptiness inside. He'd be here beside you, every step. It's easy to see he isn't.

Who shall separate you from the love of Christ? Shall trouble or hardship or persecution . . . ?

Fool. How could you believe such a ridiculous thing, after what happened to your mother?

The dreadful voice in her head drowned out every other sound, every other thought, as she stood alone in the snow.

Her cheeks were wet from crying. She turned back toward the house and toward the bedroom where her husband would keep his back toward her, pretending to sleep. Her breath came as mere wisps of frost. And her heart broke in the icy darkness.

The Fairlane

Harry Harkin lay wide-awake in his bed for the third night in a row.

Why can't I stop thinking, Lord? Why won't my mind shut down for a while?

He couldn't look at his daughter, imagining all those gauze bandages he knew were wrapped around her chest and her heart like armor, without thinking of Edna, of Edna's bandages, Edna's faith, Edna dying.

Harry didn't have to reach for the clock. When he woke up like this, he always knew the time. Three a.m. Right on the money.

Last night when he'd been jolted out of sleep, he'd been stupid enough to punch the button. The clock spoke aloud, a woman's tinny electronic voice, a clock he'd bought at K-Mart because he was getting old and he couldn't see in the dark without finding his spectacles.

"The time is three-oh-three a.m."

This time he didn't ask the confounded thing again.

He knew.

For six weeks after his wife had died, Harry had forbidden himself to touch anything that had belonged to her. He left her belongings right where she'd arranged them, small cherished altars that kept him feeling close to Edna even after she'd gone. The small blue jar of Vicks VapoRub on her nightstand. A basket of Betsy McCall paper dolls. The crumpled hanky that still smelled of Emeraude. As if she'd come back for it tomorrow, poke it in her pocketbook, laugh at him for thinking she might not need it anymore.

Then had come the day when he couldn't bear her belongings sitting around their home anymore. He'd swept through the house like a drill sergeant, his anger and grief so tangible and hard that he'd taken no prisoners. Sweep, into the box everything went. Family photos that she'd loved. Notes from the children. The grocery list he'd kept like a shrine on the counter, the last one she had scribbled in her own hand. Laundry detergent. Ground beef. Toilet paper.

Gone.

And then there was a scripture, something she'd jotted and posted on the icebox about a bird. He still remembered it, no matter how many years he'd tried to forget. "There, in your weakness, you will find the wings of the wind."

He tossed everything that made it seem as if Edna might be coming back. Into that box it went. All of it. He'd scrounged around on the laundry-room shelves, searching for packing tape, and when he couldn't find anything better, he'd taped the box shut with electrical tape. He wanted this sealed. Finished. Over-and-done-with.

Lord, why the urge to see what's inside the box now? Why, after all these years?

He'd endured this anger, this grief. He'd made precarious peace with his Heavenly Father, if only to find his way back to a place of somewhat baffled acceptance.

Wouldn't digging through her personal effects open every wound again? Can't I keep those old things sealed in the recesses of my heart? *I know myself, Father. If I let myself relive that now, I'm going to lose all hope I still have for Theia.*

He reached toward the nightstand and thumped the button on the clock.

"The time is three-oh-two a.m."

A shadow flitted past his window. Harry sat up and fumbled for his bifocals. He saw Theia trudging through the snow toward the parsonage. He watched as she backhanded her nose with a mitten.

The time is now. His heart pulsed to him in its underlying, faultless rhythm. *The time is now. The time is now.*

None of us can go on like this, Father. What is it that you want me to do?

That afternoon so long ago, he'd backed the Fairlane out of the garage, propped up the ladder, and stowed Edna's things as far back as he could get them in the corner of the attic. He'd moved that box with him three times. He hadn't unfastened it or looked inside it once.

It sat waiting in a corner of the shed beneath four or five other cardboard cartons from his household that he hadn't needed when he'd moved here with Theia and Joe.

No sense in mistaking an old man's folly for the Spirit of the Lord.

He asked the question aloud in the darkness, his forehead still pressed up against the cold windowpane. "You want me to open all that up again, Lord? Sure don't see what good it'll do anybody."

Silence.

No reassuring voice in the darkness.

Only the dull aching of his heart, the memory of the day when he'd stomped through room after room, on a crusade to purge every painful recollection, every broken promise, from his household and his life.

He watched Theia go to her house, her hand nudging the screen as it opened and then fingering it behind her so it wouldn't bang shut and awaken her family.

Was I wrong then, Lord? It hurt so badly, having you take Edna the way you did.

Best thing to do was to get it over as fast as we could and then bring us both back to an even keel with you.

I wanted to protect her, God. I didn't want my little girl to have to hurt as much as I did.

Harry settled himself into the old La-Z-Boy in the corner, folded his spectacles, and laid them beside him on the table.

· ·

Joe fanned out the pages of his sermon notes across his desk the next morning and tried to make sense of them. He scrubbed his eyes with his palms, picked up his pen and made a note. Then he stared at what he'd written for a full fifteen seconds before he shook his head, drew a line through the entire thing, pitched the pen across his desk.

The backbone of his Sunday message. Gibberish. He'd worked on this for hours, and now it made no sense at all.

She said she didn't need me for a pastor. She said she needed me for a husband.

I'm a failure at being a husband for her, Lord.

I don't know what to say to give her strength. I don't know what to say to let her know how much I love her. Even when I do think I know what to say, I open my mouth and the wrong words come out.

Stupid words. Hurtful words.

What good are you, Husband, if you have forgotten to rely on the one who seeks you for his bride?

He picked up the pages of his sermon one by one, scanned them, crumpled them into wads, and flung them against the wall.

Who am I to think I can teach anybody about you?

Who am I, that I've taken responsibility for shepherding your flock?

Have I taken responsibility, or have you given it to me, Lord?

Joe stood in the middle the office where he'd counseled hundreds, waiting, his breath coming in short laborious wheezes, his own heart an empty cavern.

He raised his fist to the ceiling, and shook it. "Show me, Father. Show me who I am!"

The room felt as empty, as cavernous as the portions of his own self that he'd finally opened up and laid out upon the winds of the heavens. Joe knew this to be true. Nothing about him was worthy or good enough or strong enough for the task that had been laid before him.

Joe lowered his arm.

He closed his eyes.

When he did, the picture came. Not so much a picture, maybe, but a living depiction. Moving figures. Wailing women gathering frightened children and herding them away. A trail of dirty, jeering Roman soldiers as they followed a bent man heaving a cross along through the dust up the hill of Golgotha.

Behind the cross stumbled this Jesus, this man they called the Christ. Joe, standing alone in his office, saw the human man as he'd never been able to see him before, heard the voices shrieking at him as he staggered onward up the hill.

"Hail, king of the Jews!" Again and again they struck him on the head with a staff. One of them ran ahead, fell on his knees, paid mocking homage to him as he passed. "Hail, king of the Jews! Oh, mighty savior of the world. If you could only save yourself now!"

Spittle coursed down his face from where they'd spat on him. Joe watched, horrified, as the soldiers lifted the cross from the shoulders of Simon and began to erect it. This then was as far as he needed to see. But even though his eyes were closed, the scene remained. He knew what would come next. They would put thorns on Jesus' head, and they would dig into his scalp and rip out his hair. They would pluck the beard from his chin until there was scarcely anything left of his face. With a cat-o-nine-tails, they would scourge him until his innards hung out of his body and his skin was shredded into tatters. They would pierce what was left of him with a spear, and his blood would begin to pour out onto the ground. His followers would desert him. His friends would betray him. Even his own Father God must turn away from him.

"No," Joe whispered. "No."

They kicked Jesus and put a bag over his head and shouted taunts. And when the bag was ripped off, this human man turned and fixed his eyes on Joe with an expression that tore his breath away. This then, he saw, was love. Love with no ulterior motive, unadulterated and true. The very definition of love, not in a dictionary, but on the cross.

"Lord," Joe cried out as this man Jesus climbed past him, onward, to his crucifixion. "Lord!"

This is how God showed his love among us: He sent his one and only Son into the world that we might live through him. This love: not that we loved God, but that he loved us and sent his Son as an atoning sacrifice for our sins.

At that moment, the room filled with a quiet gentle presence, a peace that vibrated in the very core of the pastor's soul.

This is who you are, Joe McKinnis. I have done these things for you. Now come to me.

Oh, it had been so long.

So long.

Come that I might bear all your burdens. Come that I might shepherd your flock, even as you agreed to shepherd mine.

Joe fell to his knees, his kneecaps making a hollow thud on the floor. He didn't care. His entire body shook. The trembling wouldn't stop, and he didn't want it to. He bowed before his Holy God, tears pouring forth from the very headwaters of his soul. "I'm so sorry. Oh, Lord, I'm so sorry. I'm sorry."

He cried out like an orphaned child. "I've tried so hard to do the right things. And I've been so wrong."

"I want to know you, Lord. I've been looking at myself, not at you. Help me to stop imitating you, Lord." He lifted his eyes to the heavens. "I'm so tired of trying to live that way. All I want is to be with you, Father. You working through me, not me trying to do the right things anymore."

Help me with Theia, Father. I don't even know where to start. She's shutting me out. I'm so afraid I'm going to lose her.

And then, he knew.

Oh, Lord. I'm sorry for being afraid. I'm sorry for being selfish. I'm sorry for counting the cost for myself when I ought to have been thinking of her instead. Oh, Father.

A knock came at his door.

Joe stumbled to his feet. He didn't take the time to straighten his shirt, fix his hair or attend to his face. He turned the knob and pulled the door open.

There stood Sarah Hodges, his secretary, with a cup of coffee. She offered it to him. "I was just cleaning out the pot," she said. And he'd thought she'd stare at him, only she didn't. Sarah was too busy taking stock of the wadded up pages of sermon that had landed in various corners of the room. She finally met his eyes. "You working on your Sunday message?"

"I *am*, oh I *am*." He said it with such vigor, he splashed coffee onto the carpet. It seemed years since he'd had this much joy, this much hope. "Do we have any Coffee Mate for this?" He looked into a brew strong enough to jump-start a Studebaker. "It's going to make my hair stand on end."

For the first time it seemed she got a good look at him. She booted one of his sermon pages out of her way and narrowed her eyes. "Your hair is already standing on end. Pastor McKinnis, are you okay?"

We're Back, Father

Number 19, the regular Teton County middle-school bus, crept past the McKinnis house at the exact same time every afternoon. Today, as the bus came around the corner and made its way up Big Trails Drive, Kate leaned across Jaycee to scrub her foggy breath off one window. "See, you guys." She pointed to the Fairlane where it sat waiting in the side yard. "I *told* you Grandpa was giving me his car. There it is."

Paul Jacobs pulled his Game Boy out of his backpack and started punching buttons. "That old thing? That drools. What a piece a junk."

"It isn't junk. My grandpa's been driving it for twenty-seven years. He put a new battery in it and everything."

Paul won some sort of victory on the Game Boy and it exploded into a mass crescendo of electronic sound. He rolled his eyes. "Like I said . . ."

"Your new car rocks, Kate." Jaycee snuck her a red Twizzler, being especially careful because they weren't supposed to share anything to eat on the bus. "Paul is just jealous."

"It's a Ford."

"F-O-R-D. Stands for Found On Road Dead."

"When I get my permit, he said he'll take me out to the elk refuge road so I can practice."

"I'll bet that car hasn't gone anywhere in ten years. It's buried in snow up past its hubcaps."

"That's because it just snowed this weekend, stupid. Grandpa drove it to the hospital last week."

The school bus hissed to a halt, the red stop sign folded out like an oar, and the huge yellow door accordioned open. "It's a piece of junk. It'll never run," Paul said as Kate gathered her belongings.

Jaycee waved. "See you later."

"Come over if you aren't doing anything."

"I will."

Kate hadn't thought to actually dig the car out of the snow until she saw the snow shovel propped up beside the shed. Hm-mmm. If she cleared off the hood, her friends could see it better. Annoying people on the school bus couldn't make any more comments about the Fairlane not going anywhere for ten years.

"Hey, Mom. I'm home." She left her backpack on the floor where she wasn't supposed to leave it, and went to the pantry to find a snack.

Her mother had left a note on the kitchen counter. "Gone to doctor. There all afternoon. Heidi @ dancing after that. Love, Mom."

Oh, yeah. It was Tuesday. The day of her mother's first chemo session. Kate jammed her mouth full of Doritos, found the broom, and hurried outside to begin her labors.

Kate started with the Fairlane's windows, the roof, and then the fenders. She stepped back to survey her work. Huge piles now loomed behind the wheels and in front of the headlights. This was going to be harder than it looked.

She hadn't scooped more than a dozen shovelfuls before her back began to ache and her thumbs to throb. She kept going anyway, slicing into the ice with the shovel blade, pitching the load off to one side, until she had the beginnings of a path.

Just let Paul Jacobs say this car won't go anywhere!

Slice. Pitch. Slice. Pitch.

I could get in and turn it on and drive all the way to Colorado if I wanted to!

The thought kept her going a long time. She had no idea how long she'd been digging when Jaycee came walking up the street toward her house. "Oh, my gosh, Kate! You're really digging out the car. Is your grandfather going to let you drive it somewhere?"

"Sure." Kate hesitated. "Sure he will. He might even let me take it on the highway if I'm careful."

"No way!"

She didn't know why it seemed so important to her to one-up Jaycee just then, but for some reason it did. "He said he would," she lied. "That's why I'm doing all this." Kate jabbed the shovel hard into the snow so it stood unaided in the middle of the path.

"You're so lucky." Jaycee pulled her stocking cap down further over her ears.

Kate dusted the snow off her mittens, satisfied. Well, mostly.

"It's your turn to spend the night here Friday night. You want to?"

A long moment passed. Jaycee didn't answer. She slumped against the fender of the Fairlane and stared off into oblivion, looking uncomfortable about something. At last she said, "I don't think I can."

"Why not?"

"You know." She shrugged easily, but Kate could tell something wasn't right. "There's always a whole lot going on."

"There's nothing going on. I'll ask Mom. She'll say it's fine. You'll see."

"I can't come over, Kate. Don't bother her about it."

Kate grew silent as she stored the shovel back in the shed and the two girls walked together toward the house. Suspicion niggled inside. She'd never invited her friend to stay over and been turned down before. She asked with great caution, "You want to come in?"

"Sure, that sounds good."

It was the right time of day to play music—her father was still working in his office at the church. Kate grabbed the Doritos bag and the bean dip from the fridge.

"Paul Jacobs was being a total jerk today on the bus." Jaycee followed Kate upstairs. She paused, and then spoke the next few words with entirely too much emphasis. "There are a lot of people being jerks right now."

"Including you?" Kate thought the question would take the sting out.

"I can't help it."

Kate shrugged, trying to push the pain away, but she couldn't do it. She tried a new subject. "Did you take notes in Miss Rainey's class today? On 'To Build A Fire'?" They'd been reading the Jack London story in English. "Tiffany kept passing me notes, and I never wrote anything down."

"I wrote down some stuff."

"If you came over Friday night, we could study for the test."

"Kate, I've already said I can't come."

"Whatever." Kate's lips contracted into a tight line of hurt. "Sorry I asked."

Jaycee turned away and fiddled with the row of first-place blue ribbons Kate had mounted on her bulletin board with pushpins. She'd won them all at the Teton County Fair, entering art projects.

Jaycee sniffed and her shoulders heaved. It took Kate about five seconds to figure out that her best friend was trying not to cry.

"You want to tell me what's going on?"

Jaycee shook her head, still toying with the ribbons. "I promised I wouldn't. It stinks."

Kate thought of her grandfather's car again, the Fairlane, out sitting in the snow, ready to cruise. Whenever things got bad, she thought of the car and it made her feel better. But even that didn't help much now. "Fine then. I wouldn't want you to break any promises."

"I told you everybody is being a jerk. Well, that means more than Paul Jacobs."

"Who does it mean?"

Jaycee turned around, drew a line with a finger beneath each eye to clear away tears without smudging mascara. "Tiffany Haas. She's having her birthday party Friday night. And she isn't inviting you."

Kate looked stunned. "She isn't? We're good friends. I had her to my birthday this year."

"I know."

"She kept passing me all those notes in Miss Rainey's class today."

"She's invited six people. And she's made us all promise that you don't find out."

It devastated Kate, everyone knowing the secret but her, being left out and alone. She could feel her face turning an angry red. "How come she doesn't want me?"

Jaycee didn't answer the question. "We're driving to Idaho Falls. Her mother's gotten us a room at the Ameritel, and we're going to spend the night and swim. We're going shopping at the mall the next day."

Kate asked the same question again. "How come she doesn't want me?"

"If you ask her to her face, she'll have an excuse."

"Which is—?"

"That there isn't room in her mom's Suburban for anybody else."

Kate tried her best not to get further disturbed. In her head, she listed the names of Tiffany's other friends, girls Kate liked, and would have wanted to shop with. It would have been so much fun to be a part of the crowd. "Maybe that's a good-enough excuse."

"It's a fine excuse. Only it isn't why."

"It isn't?"

"It's because of your mother, Kate. Because she has cancer. Tiffany didn't invite you because she's worried you might talk about your mother's cancer. Her mom agreed with her. She thought it wouldn't be fair, asking you to have fun when there was something so sad happening to your family. Tiffany's mother said she wouldn't know what to say."

Theia pushed herself up off the couch in the waiting area and watched through the one-way mirror in studio three as Heidi danced. She was doing her best to keep up with the other clowns, but it would take weeks for her to grasp this complicated routine. Even so, she bounded around the room to the strains of Tchaikovsky as if she'd been given a gift, springing forward in the circle and catching hands, grinning when she made a misstep, catching hands, trying it over.

At one point when she made a mistake, Heidi gestured with wild animation toward her teacher. The instructor nodded. Theia watched as everyone took hands again, circled once, broke the circle, and then whipped into it backwards. The teacher pursed her lips and tilted her chin, then began slowly nodding again. "That's great," Theia could read her words through the glass. "Let's add it to the dance."

Theia stood in the hallway, the way she'd stood so many times before, her hand barely resting on the temporary cotton prosthesis beneath her blouse. Somewhere deep in her belly, the queasiness and the exhaustion that the doctor had predicted had begun.

She had wanted to scream when she'd undergone her first chemotherapy, but there hadn't been anyone to scream at. Other people sat in the waiting room with friends, but Theia had not allowed anyone to come.

In the chemo room, they'd placed a blue ice bag on her head, supposed to prevent her hair from falling out by freezing the roots, the nurse had explained while she worked a needle into Theia's arm. Then Dr. Sugden entered and started the IV drip, first something called Kytril to stop the nausea, then the second, a red Kool-Aid liquid that made her vibrate like a stringed instrument from the inside out. They told her that for the first several treatments at least, the sick feeling would dissipate before much time passed. No one could tell her exactly how her body would respond, what to expect. They'd sent her home with a list of printed instructions that she'd tucked inside her purse. She was to call the nurse if she developed fever over 101, started bleeding or bruising, or if the nausea didn't go away.

At Dancers' Workshop, Julie Stevens came down the hall behind her and stopped to watch. "The steps to this one are difficult for her, Mrs. McKinnis," she murmured. "I hope she doesn't get discouraged."

The hours had worn on last night, sleep eluding Theia yet again, the anxiety building and making her frantic as the hours passed.

Why couldn't she tell Joe how frightened she was?

Inside the studio, the instructor had started them on cartwheels. Heidi moved across the floor like a gigantic broken turtle, shaking her head and laughing, trying to get her hands on the floor and her feet in the air.

This morning, Dr. Sugden had informed Theia that although having cancer wouldn't make her look gray and shaky, having treatments would. Her friends and family would easily confuse symptoms of the treatment with symptoms of the disease.

Even though Heidi couldn't hear, Theia whispered the same cartwheel directions her own mother had given her, out in a grassy yard, somewhere long ago.

Hand. Hand. Foot. Foot.

Come on, Heidi. You can do it.

Hand. Hand. Foot. Foot.

The door opened upstairs. Four or five little girls came tramping down the wooden steps, their booted feet clattering as they came.

Julie Stevens took a pen from behind her ear and jotted something down. "Do you want to be a volunteer for the Christmas performances, Mrs. McKinnis? If you do, I'll put your name on the list."

Theia thought about her answer for a moment, and then smiled. "Yes. I'd like that very much."

It certainly hadn't taken much time, getting Tiffany and Megan over to her house. "I know about your birthday, Tiffany." Kate planted her hands on her hips and flipped her hair over her shoulder. "Next time your mother doesn't want me to come to something, you can just tell me. You don't have to talk to everybody else in school first."

Tiffany tilted her head toward Jaycee. "You've got a big mouth, you know that?"

"I can't help it. Kate's my best friend."

"I trusted you."

"If you didn't want me to tell Kate, you shouldn't have invited me in the first place."

Tiffany squared her hands on her hips, too. "Well, maybe I'm sorry that I did."

After all the hurt and disappointment, Kate now did her best to become the peacemaker. "It's okay, Tiffany. I made her tell me. I bugged her and bugged her until she'd say what was going on."

Jaycee didn't back down. "I'm going to stay here Friday night and spend the night with Kate."

"Fine. You do whatever you want to do. The rest of us are going where we can have fun. Nothing fun ever happens around this place."

Megan Spence, who had been flipping through CDs in the corner, gave out a little laugh. "Tiffany. You're wrong. Of course there's fun stuff to do here. Kate has her own car."

"Yeah," Jaycee echoed.

"So what?" Tiffany was gathering up her things to go. "She can't drive it yet."

"Yeah. But I can," Megan said.

All the girls stared. She waved her billfold in the air. "I've got my hardship license right here."

Kate's heart froze.

"So." Tiffany slid her arms into her coat. "Why are we all sitting around here? Let's go somewhere."

"We can't do that." Kate's heart was now pounding out of her chest.

"Why not? It's your car, isn't it?"

"Yes, but I haven't—"

"You've been bragging about it for days."

"I know, but it's not the way I've made it sound."

"Whatever."

"Where can we go?"

"The library?"

"We can't make any noise at the library."

"I could get a book for my book report, though."

"We could drive up and down the elk refuge road and listen to KMTN."

"We could go to Dairy Queen."

By the time they'd all chimed in, Kate could not figure out how to say no. Only Jaycee glanced back at her with some hint of remorse as they went outside, looking in every direction to make sure that nobody was watching them. Megan started up the car.

"Where's your grandpa?" Jaycee asked as Megan backed out.

"I don't know."

Kate fingered the door handle. A piece of silver peeled off beneath her nail. The inside of the precious Fairlane smelled musty and old.

It wasn't supposed to be like this. It was supposed to be something special that Grandpa and I did together.

"Where's your dad?"

"In his office. He's got counseling appointments and stuff."

They stopped at the sign on the corner of Big Trails and made a right onto the highway. In Harry Harkin's old Ford Fairlane, the four young girls hit the open road.

"Turn on the radio!"

"It's cold back here. Can you turn on the heater?"

"Just a minute! I have to figure out how to turn everything on." Megan pressed the dial on the radio, and it took a few seconds to warm up and start playing. "Kate, this car is really old."

"I know that."

They passed the turnoff to High School Road where the middle school and the high school sat side by side. They passed McDonald's, the Wyoming Inn, the pawnshop, and the Sagebrush Motel.

"I hate that song. Can you change it?"

"Where are we going?"

"Did anyone bring any money?"

They ended up at Dairy Queen. They pooled all their change and had enough to buy one Blizzard. They doubled back and had driven halfway to the Moose-Wilson Road when Megan glanced over her shoulder at Kate and grinned. "It's your turn. You want to try?"

"Me?"

"It's your car, isn't it?"

Tiffany laughed nervously. "She can't drive, Megan. You're being crazy."

Jaycee sat beside Kate, her fists clenched at her sides, not saying a word.

Kate stared at her friend, her pulse drumming in her throat. She squirmed in her seat, more than uncomfortable. Megan had pulled over to the side, and they were all looking at her.

I can handle everything that everybody's throwing at me. "Well, it isn't a big deal," Kate said at last, mostly to Jaycee. "If Megan can drive, so can I."

"You can?"

"Sure."

Megan turned around again and eyed her from the front seat. "Kate, you're such a goodie goodie. A preacher's kid. You know you don't really want to drive this thing."

"Yes, I do."

For what seemed an eternity, nobody moved. Tiffany finally flipped down the sun visor, opened her little pot of Carmex and used the mirror to smear some across her mouth. "Well, you're right, it's not that big a deal. Everybody's tried it by now," she said casually. "Cheri Fraser walked home one day when her mom had gone to Idaho Falls and drove us up to Yellowstone. We were gone all day."

"Driving ought to be easy," Jaycee said.

"You really want to try?" Megan's eyes met hers in the rearview mirror.

"Yes."

Kate had thought her positive answer would send them running from the car screaming. But it didn't. They sat right where they were, except for Megan, who got out and gestured for Kate to scoot in behind the steering wheel. "Go ahead. I'll teach you."

Kate climbed out of the back seat, came around, and slid inside. She put her hands on the steering wheel. The car had suddenly grown ten times bigger. She leaned against the bench seat and felt the ancient upholstery crackle beneath her. She checked the rearview mirror, but all she could see were her own eyebrows, her own pale forehead. She blew out a breath. "I don't think I want to do this."

"Just turn it on. Put the car in gear and it'll go forward. That's all there is to it."

From where Kate sat, she could see Tiffany Haas stretching her arm along the ledge beside the window and flicking her nails against the register where the heat flowed.

Tiffany, who hadn't wanted Kate at her overnight party because having her might spoil the fun.

At this one moment, driving this car became a declaration of liberty for her, a way to show the whole world, God included, that she could handle growing up.

I don't need my mother! I can do things on my own.

Kate turned the key. The engine roared to life at first try.

It felt incredible sitting here, a powerful engine throbbing beneath the hood, as if Kate controlled the whole world.

"Put your foot on the brake first. Then you put it in drive."

Which one was drive? Kate manhandled the shift and moved the red line to "R," which she decided must stand for "regular." They rolled backwards, bumping up over the curb.

"No. No! That's reverse," three girls hollered to her all at once. "Put it on the 'D.' That's drive. That makes you go forward."

She pulled the stick down, felt a clunk beneath her, and jumped.

"You're doing fine. Fine. Now press down on the accelerator. That other pedal down there."

"There's another pedal?" Almost as fast as she asked the question, she found it with her foot. The Fairlane lurched forward. Jaycee grabbed the door handle. Megan screamed.

Just try to take my mother away, God. Do what you want to do, but you can't scare me!

She thought she was laughing, but then she realized she was choking on her tears. Her chest heaved, expanding for the air it wasn't getting.

"You're driving in the bike lane."

She yanked the wheel and went too far, jerking the car left, across the yellow line into the turn lane.

"Put the car in Park, Kate. Put it on the 'P.'"

A pick-up truck loomed in the turn lane, coming right at them. They all three screeched. "Move over, Kate!"

She had to crane over her right shoulder to check the lane. A Suburban roared past. "I can't."

Brakes squealed. For precious seconds, Kate sought the brakes in the Fairlane and found only air.

Bumpers came together in a terrifying crunch of metal. The girls pitched forward. Gravel flew.

When the car stopped, Kate moved the red line to "P."

She ignored the tears of frustration and defeat as they coursed down her cheeks. Instead, she switched the key off like an expert, and sat taller.

Kate

In Harry Harkin's humble opinion, the Lord had blessed him two-fold. First, he'd given him a passel of coffee-drinking buddies who would help him dig through the bizarre assortment of items stashed in the storage shed, carrying things out voluntarily and without complaint. Second, those very same coffee-drinking buddies asked no questions and left him alone when the time came to strip off the tape and see inside the old dusty box.

Harry had never been one for tearing up good boxes. He retrieved a table knife from the drawer in his little kitchenette, made one clean slice through the right end of the box, then the left. At last he cut across the center seam in the box, making a clean dissection. He laid the knife beside him on the carpet, and steeled his heart against what he knew he would find inside.

He expected to throw open the panels of cardboard and have the scent, the very essence of Edna, come pouring out at him. But it didn't. Instead, when he bent back the lid of the box, everything inside smelled bitter and brittle, decayed with age. He leaned away and frowned.

How fresh and painful these treasures had been once, so long ago. How old and lost they seemed to him now.

He sat high on his old haunches, allowing himself—for the briefest of moments—to feel cheated. For this, he could blame no one but himself. He'd discovered that there could be no hurrying the grieving process. Sealing this box, its contents, had been his one desperate attempt to contain an unbearable, devastating hurt, a hurt that had proven impossible to tame.

Harry had journeyed in its shadow for a lifetime.

Would that he had not locked away these memories, these precious belongings of the woman who'd slept beside him and held him and nursed him and encouraged him for thirty-one years.

Would that he had touched these and cherished them while they still bore the fresh scent of her, the recent grip of her hand, the rare allusion of her presence.

Harry edged close again, and with a sense of desperation, peered inside.

Lord, will you show me? What is it that you intend for me to find here?

With one tentative hand, he began to remove items from the box.

Edna's favorite red housedress. A tiny bowl she'd kept on the kitchen windowsill, where she laid her wedding rings when she took them off to wash the dishes. Her darning thimble, kept in the wooden sewing basket beside her feet, worn so thin that daylight shone through the tin where she'd used it. The monogrammed mint-green towel he'd found in the bathroom the day of her funeral, right where she'd left it, folded and lopped over the side of the tub. He lifted it high, let it fall open, seeking Edna.

He found only dust.

Harry refolded the towel and laid it aside with her other things. He reached in again. Touched leather. And knew.

Edna had always loved the feel of this Bible. He'd watched her when it was new, balancing it in one hand and running a palm over it with her other, enjoying the limber weight of it, the gold foiled pages, the way, when she dropped it open, it fell right to a place in the middle of Psalms.

He held it in both hands and stared at it.

It's only her Bible, after all. This is no surprise. I've known it was here ever since I closed that box.

Harry couldn't put it down. He saw Edna then, in his mind's eye, and the sight of her made his heart spiral up to his throat. He viewed her as clearly as if someone had shown him a picture of her, every feature of her face distinct, the sewing box open beside her ankles while she rocked, the heavy Bible open in her lap, her smile a portent of peace. He remembered how she read every page of this book as if it was a treasure, lifting the page from the bottom right-hand corner, turning it slowly, smoothing the center of the leather-bound volume with the flat of her hand.

Father. He thought it, prayed it, the way he often called upon the name of his God. Is this how you've meant it to be, then? That I was trained once with my wife so I could better minister to Joe, and to Theia most of all?

The Bible plopped open, as if to answer him.

When he glanced down, expecting Psalms, he found something more. An onionskin blue envelope with pink rosebuds, vaguely familiar, with scalloped edges, like lace.

Harry was afraid to touch it. He remembered Edna had such stationery once. He remembered her writing notes to her parents on it.

He turned over the envelope. What he saw made chills run up his spine.

"To Theia," it read in Edna's bold, slanted script.

In his own mind Harry began to play devil's advocate, thinking of all the reasons this letter might not be what it appeared to be. Perhaps this letter had already been opened. Perhaps it was something Theia had already read, something day-to-day and fun and childlike, not significant at all. Perhaps Edna had kept it tucked inside her own Bible for years, simply as a remembrance.

Harry flipped the envelope over again and checked the flap.

Still sealed.

Harry's chest went tight. He understood the full truth. Theia had not read this letter.

She might never have seen it, if not for his digging in the box.

Emotion clogged his throat, misted his eyes. Harry closed the Bible, leaving it exactly as he'd found it, so his daughter could discover the envelope the same way he had discovered it.

He laid Edna's Bible with great care on the floor beside him.

Then he rocked back on his heels and whispered words of praise and gratefulness up to the sky.

Theia had just slammed the car door, opened the hatch of the Subaru, and tried to bring in too many grocery bags at once. She lugged them to the kitchen counter, dug for the medication they'd given her, put away the new gallon of milk, and reminded Heidi to hang her dance bag on a peg in the utility room.

She saw that Harry was in his greenhouse again, no doubt watering the tiny sprouts of his paper white bulbs as they nudged up, green and fragile, from the soil.

Neither Harry nor any of the McKinnises had happened around to the side yard or noticed that the Ford Fairlane was gone.

The phone rang in Joe's office. He clenched the receiver against his ear and listened while the officer gave him sparse details of the crash.

Kate had been involved in an accident. There had been a number of young girls in the car. It had collided head-on with another vehicle.

"She's at the police station. She isn't at the hospital?"

"She wasn't injured, Mr. McKinnis. But one of the other girls has been taken to the emergency room with cuts on her knee."

As he ran across the snow-covered yard toward the house, he stopped and pounded on the greenhouse door. "Dad, did you see Kate leave with anybody this afternoon? Did a friend come over and pick her up?"

"No. I"—Harry shot a fleeting look out over the road beside them—"I've been doing something else."

Joe ran next to his own house. "Theia, did you hear from Kate? Did she leave you a note or anything?"

Theia moved several grocery bags and checked the kitchen table, where they always left notes for each other if need be. "Nope. Nothing here. Where is she, Joe? Is something wrong?"

"I'll tell you on our way into town."

Heidi started yanking her coat back on. "Can I go, too?"

Joe shook his head. "Your grandpa's working in his greenhouse. Go knock on his door and tell him you need to stay with him for a little while."

All was decided. Joe backed out of the driveway, bumping over the wedge of snow that the plow left every time it cleared the road.

"Are you going to tell me what all this is about?"

"Kate has been in a car accident."

"No. Oh, Joe, is she hurt?"

"Apparently not. Who was she with, Theia? Why didn't she leave a note to tell you she was going somewhere?"

"I have no idea. She's always so good about that."

"She was with some friend. Jaycee, maybe? I don't know who else would have come over after school."

"Joe, I—" Theia leaned her head back against the seat. The nausea she'd been battling all afternoon came upon her full bore. Her stomach roiled. "Joe, I'm going to be sick."

He pulled over for her, yanked the door open, leaned over her and held her head while she gave in to the effects of chemotherapy. She retched onto the graveled shoulder, gasping for air. "We've got to get there."

"We're okay, Theia." This time, his words didn't sound empty at all. He meant them. "She's waited for us already. She can wait a little bit longer." Joe searched the car for something she could wipe her face on. He found a pack of wet wipes in the glove compartment. When Theia sat up and leaned against the headrest, he folded one of them to make a cool compress. He pressed it against her forehead, her temple, her other temple.

"Thanks," she whispered with a weak smile. "That's been coming on all afternoon."

"Are you okay to go?"

She closed her eyes, nodded. "Yeah."

They drove another three blocks, his knuckles white knobs as he clenched the wheel. Then, in one abrupt motion, he steered them off to the right again and pushed the emergency brake on.

She stared at him. "Joe? What's happening?"

For a long moment, he stared at his hands. Then he turned to her, spoke aloud to her the things he had given over to his Holy Father earlier. "Theia, I'm so sorry for so many things."

When she answered, he heard the hurt edge into her voice. "I don't think this is exactly the time we need to be discussing this."

"Perhaps it isn't. But we must discuss it soon." He took her hands. "Right now, there's something else more important."

She lifted her eyes to his. "What is that?"

"We must pray. Together."

He saw her jaw go tight, saw the line of her lips begin to stiffen, and then to tremble.

"I know." He touched her face, touching all the pain that he knew she still carried. "I know," he whispered, as he took her hands in his. He pulled them to him, entwined his fingers with hers, held them there.

"I can't pray," she said, shaking her head.

He didn't let her go. "You want to tell me about it?"

She shook her head. "He wouldn't want to listen to me."

"He would. He *does*."

"I don't think God cares about me, Joe. How could a God who cares about his children let cancer come into their lives?"

"I've seen it, Theia. I've felt it. He's made me to understand his love better than I've ever understood it before."

"I can't see it. I can't feel it."

"What he feels about his children having cancer, he took to the cross."

"If he died on the cross for me, he died for my sins, Joe, not for my cancer."

"All I know is this, Theodore. On that cross, he rendered evil ineffective. He took it upon himself, and then he crushed it. Disease, sin, bad things—they haven't ceased to exist, but their power has been broken. Your cancer has not been abolished, but overthrown."

Her fingers curled into the safety of his hand. She stared at them there.

He joined her gaze, staring at his larger fingers covering hers, their fingers wrought together like sinews of rope.

At last she spoke. "I was so wrong to not let you come with me today."

"I'll come the next time," he said. "And the next and the next and the next. I am your husband. I want to be there."

Her two words, only a slight whisper. "Thank you."

"Will you pray with me for Kate, Theia?"

She nodded, tears in her eyes. "Yes, I will."

For the first time since the diagnosis, they bent heads side by side, rearranged their clasped hands. "Holy God," Joe whispered, speaking aloud. "Protect our daughter. Keep her from harm. We can't do it, Lord, but we know you can. Surround her with your angels. And give us renewed wisdom. Help us to know what to say, where to turn, when we see her. Amen."

"Amen," Theia said too and squeezed his hand.

Thanksgivings

The fluorescent bulb glared above the sergeant's metal desk, washing it in sterile, harsh light. Kate sat in a wooden chair in one corner, rocking even though the chair was stationary, her hands trapped between her knees.

"Sergeant Ray Howard," his nametag read.

"Which one of you"—Joe wrapped one arm around his wife and held her next to him—"is going to tell us what's going on?"

Kate stared at her knees.

Sergeant Howard flipped a felt-tip pen and caught it midair. "That ought to be up to your daughter, Pastor McKinnis. It seems she has a few important details that she needs to pass along."

"And those details are—?" He stared at his daughter.

The sergeant flipped his pen again. "We couldn't find any insurance information in the glove compartment, for one thing."

Theia moved over and spoke to their daughter in a gentle, urging voice, the same way a child might urge a kitten down out of a tree. "Kate, will you tell us what happened?"

Joe's eyes were locked on the officer behind the desk. "What do you mean, you couldn't find any insurance information in the glove compartment? What glove compartment?"

"The glove compartment of that antique contraption your daughter calls a car."

Still the truth did not sink in. "Our insurance ought not to have to be responsible. Whoever was *driving* ought to be responsible. Whoever owns the *car* ought to be responsible."

Sergeant Howard gave an exasperated little chuff of breath. His look at Kate said it all: "It's in your court now, girl." He shrugged at Kate.

She said it so softly they almost couldn't hear her.

"I was driving, Dad."

Stunned silence. Then, "What? What were you driving?"

"Grandpa's car."

Joe looked at Theia. How had they had not noticed that the old Fairlane was gone? It had sat forever in plain sight, at the side of the house, where anyone walking past could see it.

Joe raked one hand through his hair. "Grandpa Harkin was going to *teach* you, Kate. He wanted to use the experience to help you grow up and become a responsible person. How could you just throw such a gift away? From someone who loves you like that? All to go joyriding—what? To impress a few friends?"

She shook her head, the tears pooling in her eyes. "I don't know, Dad. I really don't."

"*Is* the car insured, Pastor McKinnis?"

"I don't know. I'll have to talk to my father-in-law about that."

Theia sank to the floor beside Kate, laying a hand of reassurance on her daughter's knee. "He doesn't have insurance on that old car, honey," she said to Joe. She turned to the officer. "It isn't a roadworthy vehicle. He had it out once, about ten days ago. But he didn't insure it. I'm sure he planned to take care of it before he gave his granddaughter driving lessons."

Sergeant Howard made a note on the clipboard. Then another. "The registration isn't up to date, either. We found that out when we ran the license plate number. It hasn't been renewed in the state of Wyoming since 1989."

"Where is the car right now?" Joe asked.

"We've got it out in the impound lot. We towed it in with damage to the left front fender. And here's a copy of the police report filed by the driver of the other vehicle." He yanked a copy of the report out of the clipboard and handed it over.

Joe took the papers without looking at them. He was staring at Kate.

Sergeant Howard ran his forehead back and forth in the flat of his hand. "So let's go over the charges, shall we? First, driving an uninsured vehicle. Second, driving a vehicle with expired tags. Third, failure to signal a lane change. Fourth, driving without a license. Usually in cases like these, where the driver has borrowed a vehicle from a member of the family, the family elects not to press charges of vehicle theft. But I—"

Joe interrupted, this time with a hint of a smile. "She's our fourteen-year-old daughter, Officer Howard. I doubt very much her grandfather will want to prosecute."

"I'll need to talk to Mr. Harkin about that, I'm afraid. Although he hasn't phoned us to report the car missing at present time."

"He doesn't know it's missing. None of us knew."

"Maybe if you kept a closer eye on your children, Pastor, these things wouldn't come as such a surprise."

Sergeant Howard slapped the clipboard on his desk the same way a judge would clap down a gavel. "She'll be scheduled to appear in Juvenile District Court two weeks from today, in front of Judge Terry Rogers. You are welcome to hire a lawyer or let Kate plead her case on her own. It makes no difference, really. The outcome is generally the same."

. . . .

Theia waited outside Kate's bedroom, her hand on the doorknob, her forehead inclined against the wooden door. Once more, she fought against the fatigue that had threatened to overcome her since their silent drive home from the police station. Faint music played inside her daughter's room.

At last she gave a timid knock, once, twice, not knowing for certain if Kate would invite her to enter.

"Hm-m-mm?" came a sleepy voice.

"Kate? It's Mom."

"Come in."

Kate was curled up in her single bed, propped up by pillows, reading a paperback novel.

"How are you doing in here?"

"Okay." Kate flipped a page of her book and kept reading.

Theia shoved her arms inside the big pockets of her bathrobe, touched one toe of her slipper to the other. "I just came to say good night. To tuck you in, if you wanted me to."

Another page turned. "You haven't tucked me in since I was eight years old."

"I know that. I thought maybe it was time we start it again."

Kate's computer screen lit the room. Her iTunes music library held a hundred songs or more. The arrow moved to the next-in-line. ZOEgirl started playing. "I don't want to talk about today, Mom."

"It's okay." Theia didn't move toward her daughter. She only stood in the middle of the room, feeling stranded. "I don't think I want to talk about it, either."

Outside, gauze clouds stretched thin across the stars, and the moon shone transparent against the sky, as though someone had tried to erase it. Theia's sense of loss settled someplace deep inside her ribcage, growing hard and heavy and cold there.

"I need to apologize to you, Kate."

"No, you don't."

"I've been a pretty crummy mom for the past few weeks."

Kate laid the book upside down, the pages forming a tent on her belly.

"You haven't been. You've been fine."

"Even though I've been in this house with you, I've been far away."

"I can understand it, really. You've had some pretty crummy things happening lately."

Despite her exhaustion, Theia finally gathered the courage to move toward her daughter and sit on the edge of the mattress. It creaked as it bore her weight. "There's no reason that you and your sister and your father should have to pay for those things right along with me."

"Yes, there is." Kate rustled around in all the pillows and blankets until she could sit straight up beside her mother. "We're your family."

Another full minute of silence passed between the two of them before Kate pitched her book on the floor and flopped back three layers of covers. She patted the bed beside her. "Would you get all the way in bed with me the way you used to do, Mama? Back in the days when we used to read stories?"

Theia touched her daughter's cheek, swallowed so hugely that they both heard it.

"I don't know if there's room for both of us anymore. I haven't done this since you were—"

"Eight years old."

"We're both bigger than we used to be."

"Doesn't make any difference."

Theia crawled into bed with her daughter, turned on her side so they fit together like spoons. The Creator had cut them from the same family cloth. Their hips fit. Their bellies and their backs curved like instruments at the same places. Their shoulder bones jutted at the same angle, shadow images like limbs of the same tree, one alongside the other.

Kate moved over to give her mother more room. Theia scrunched around until she got the comforter adjusted. The bed felt wonderful. At last she could give in to the weariness that sapped her strength.

"Knock, knock," Kate whispered into the darkness.

"Who's there?"

"Little old lady."

"Little old lady who?"

"That's funny. I didn't know you could yodel."

Theia shook her head and chuckled.

"Didn't you get it? Little old lady who."

"I got it."

"I have another one."

"I'm almost afraid to ask."

"What did Snow White say when she took her film in to be developed?"

Theia couldn't help herself. She started to giggle. "I don't know. What did Snow White say?"

"She said, 'Someday my *prints* will come.' Get it? My *prints*."

They couldn't help themselves after that, both dissolved in helpless laughter.

They laughed until it hurt, pressing their faces into the pillows to keep from waking everybody else. They laughed until they cried. When they finally flopped over backwards, bellies sore and hearts lighter than they'd been in weeks, Theia rested her fingers on top of Kate's head.

She experienced, at that moment, an almost excruciating sense of the beauty, the texture, of life. She combed through silky strands of Kate's hair, reveling in the blend of its colors together, chicory brown and golden, a sheen like water. She smelled the fragrance of her daughter, sweet and fresh, like field clover tossed by a breeze. Even the bed linens exploded onto her senses, the entwining of the cotton threads, crisp and soft at the same time, a gift.

She thought of Heidi dancing in the studio, skipping across wooden honey floors, laughing at her missteps, her hair tucked behind one ear, her body pirouetting with joyful abandon before the mirrors.

The girls were each so beautiful and young and talented and . . . and *blessed.*

The world, and all of heaven, awaited her daughters.

How dearly she loved the two of them. She loved them fiercely, completely, to a depth that proved unbearable.

I have loved you with an everlasting love, Theia. I have drawn you with loving kindness.

Her entire body quickened. Here, in this quiet place, lying in bed with her daughter, she could hear without distraction or debate. No other voices plagued her. Only the gentle, quiet declaration that delved deep, winnowed her spirit to its very core.

Beloved.

He came to her, an almost audible voice out of the stars and the darkness and the breeze outside the window. Her spirit rose up in response to the waves of warm certainty and love that enveloped her spirit. Her heart waited, poised, for an answer.

Lord? Lord, is that you?

His answer didn't come in the form she'd expected. It came as the seed of something deep and new, a jewel of wisdom, embedded securely in her soul.

All at once she understood something about herself that she hadn't understood before. She now held in her hand a freeing truth.

In the midst of her struggle with cancer, she'd spent the last weeks methodically counting the cost in her life. The time had come now to take the same careful account of every blessing.

Theia wound a strand of Kate's hair around her pointer finger, unwound it, and rewound it again.

I'm afraid, Lord.

Let go.

Father, it scares me to let go.

My arms will catch you. My arms will hold you. Don't you know?

I know, but I don't know. Sometimes it seems so hard to believe.

Joe had said there are times when the most eloquent prayers to the Father are the ones that contain no words. Theia took a deep breath, reveling as the air rushed into her lungs. Surely she wasn't alone. None of this had to be faced alone anymore. She didn't have to figure it out or understand it. She curled up in the bed beside Kate and gave herself up, gave up all the burdens of her heart, her shame, her terror, her anger, her faithlessness, to the Heavenly Father who already knew her heart to its very center.

And as she did, she knew something else. She knew her Lord's love. She felt him holding her. She grasped the knowledge for the thousandth time and for the first time. She tasted how wide and how long and how high and deep was his love for her. He loved her, cared for her, more than her husband or her own daughters. All those earthly blessings, only a reflection of the love that he wanted her to know from the depths and the heights of heaven.

The love for her that he had carried to the cross.

After a long while she whispered, "Kate, I'm so glad to be your mother."

Kate nestled even closer against her in the single bed. "I'm glad you're my mom, too." A long pause, then, "I know why I drove

Grandpa's car today. I drove it to show you how independent I could be. I drove it to show that, no matter what happens with you, I can manage on my own."

"Your dad and I both know you're growing up." But this went much deeper than just recognizing that Kate was maturing, and Theia knew it. "I'm here for you, sweetie. You can talk about all this stuff with me."

"I get really scared, Mom, when I think that something might happen to you."

It was what Theia had expected all along. *Put the right words in my mouth, Father. Please. I don't know what to say to her about this.*

Magically, miraculously, the words began almost to speak themselves. "Growing up doesn't mean that you have to grow independent, Kate. God wants you to rely on him, no matter what happens. He wants you to know that, no matter how difficult things become, you'll never have to manage on your own."

Goosebumps raised on Theia's arms. She had no idea where any of this was coming from. *It's what you want me to learn, too, isn't it, Father?*

"I want to do that, Mom. I want to trust that much in the Lord."

"Oh, Kate, so do I."

It's so hard to let go, Father. Show me how. Saying something and doing something are two such different things.

Again her heart waited, poised, listening. Again the Father answered Theia in a different way than she'd expected. In the midst of her asking to be shown, the Heavenly Father was already showing her.

He was using her to teach the lesson to someone else.

Ribbons and Rings

The morning of Thanksgiving, and the living room at the McKinnis household had been transformed into a room for a family feast. Early, while overzealous, overdressed television stars gave viewers a blow-by-blow description of the floats in the Cotton Bowl parade, Joe added both leaves to their huge country oak table. He found his wife in the kitchen in her bathrobe, wrestling with the turkey and getting it ready to go into the pan.

He kissed the back of her neck, almost liking the idea that he no longer had to move her mantle of hair to do so. Since her hair had come out, first in strands and then in clumps, Joe had fallen in love with new parts of his wife that he hadn't seen before, the hollow at the base of her skull that perfectly fit the shape of his thumb, the swan arch of her spine that made her seem so beautiful and strong. He loved the way she wore gypsy-colored scarves knotted to look like flowers on her head. He enjoyed noticing her vast array of earrings.

And, for Christmas, he had already decided to give her diamonds. Yeah, he could afford it.

"Hey," she said. He could feel her smiling even though he couldn't see her expression. "You want to open the oven door for this bird?"

He'd forgotten, until he saw Theia struggle with the heavy roaster, that her pectoral muscle didn't work so well these days. "Here. Let me get that. You're trying to do too much."

"No, I'm not. Everybody's helping."

Indeed, they were. The girls would be up in no time, and clamoring to get started on the pumpkin cake. Everyone that they'd invited to share in this day had insisted on bringing something—cranberry salad, mashed potatoes and gravy, fresh green beans, sweet potato pie. Only he'd heard Theia telling everyone in no uncertain terms that she could not be persuaded to give up cooking the McKinnis family turkey.

"Theodore. Promise me you'll lay down today and rest if you need to."

"I promise." She pecked him on the nose. "Thank you for agreeing to let me do this crazy thing."

"Not many people give huge holiday parties while they're battling cancer."

"I know that. But I want to see everyone."

"It's going to be a wonderful Thanksgiving," he said.

"More wonderful"—a jangle of earrings punctuated her joy—"because this year I truly realize how much we have to be thankful for."

· ·

Because so many had insisted on helping Theia with the food, she'd been left free to arrange her table as she pleased. She'd sent

Edna's antique-lace tablecloth off to Blue Spruce cleaners to be pressed. This morning, she unfolded it and arranged the lace just as she wanted across the dark grain of the wood. At each place she set an index card with goofy turkey and pilgrim stickers. On each card, at each place, she'd written a different scripture.

"Therefore, since we are receiving a kingdom that cannot be shaken, let us be thankful, and so worship God acceptable with reverence and awe" (Hebrews 12:28).

"Give thanks to the Lord, call on his name; make known among the nations what he has done" (1 Chronicles 16:8).

"Enter his gates with thanksgiving and his courts with praise; give thanks to him and praise his name. For the Lord is good and his love endures forever; his faithfulness continues through all generations" (Psalm 100:4–5).

She stepped back and inspected her handiwork. The goblets, polished and gleaming, were ready for iced tea. A gift from Joe's mother one November, the candlesticks stood tall and proud, a Mr. and Mrs. Pilgrim bedecked in early-American finery.

Theia came to her own chair, the seat closest to the kitchen where she could jump up to retrieve condiments and refills when necessary. She set the card beside her goblet and read her verses for the umpteenth time.

"Let your gentleness be evident to all. The Lord is near. Do not be anxious about anything, but in everything, by prayer and petition, with thanksgiving, present your requests to God. And the peace of God, which transcends all understanding, will guard your hearts and your minds in Christ Jesus" (Philippians 4:5–7).

On the television, the Rose Bowl parade ended and football began. Everyone would be arriving soon. Kate and Heidi were arguing at the counter over who got to lick the icing beaters.

Not thirty minutes later, the doorbell began to ring. The parsonage filled with guests within the hour. Harry arrived carrying a huge basket of chrysanthemums to place beside the hearth, an assortment of breads from The Bunnery, and a gift, wrapped the way he always swathed his packages, in ancient tissue paper tied with string. Before Theia had the chance to ask him about it, Sarah Hodges drove up with her family. Next came Winston Taylor, who shook Joe's hand roundly and hugged both of the girls.

Jaycee appeared at the door with her parents, Lois and Tom Maxwell, and her two little brothers. "Happy Thanksgiving!" Joe welcomed them, and took their coats at the door.

"Oh, Theia. What a beautiful table. Look at the scriptures at each place."

"Everything's so pretty."

"We made the cake." Kate held up a beater.

"And everything smells so good!"

Not one person walked through the door without bearing a dish of something wonderful. Cakes and pies and casseroles vied for position on the buffet, then overflowed onto the coffee table. The very sight of so much food, the aromas, the ingredients, the hearts and hands that had prepared the meal, set Theia's senses to reeling. She'd been having a difficult time eating since chemotherapy started. Even when the nausea subsided, she battled with a metallic tang that stayed in her mouth for days. She lowered herself into a chair in the dining room, gripping the back of it for support.

Lord, help me to be open and aware today. In the midst of my thankfulness, help me to be vulnerable and real. That's what you want from me, and I know it.

Eleanor Taggart sat beside her and touched her knee. "What can I do for you today, Theia?"

On her lips were her automatic response, "Nothing. Everything's taken care of." But Theia realized that wasn't what she was meant to say at all. She thought for a moment and came up with something. "When the timer buzzes, will you take the dressing out of the turkey for me? Before Joe carves."

"I can do that."

"Thanks, Eleanor. For the time being, just sit and talk while I get my bearings, okay? All this food, and I could use a little conversation."

"Yes. I will." A light, gentle smile. "How have you been?"

Theia had begun to understand, during these past weeks, that this was the way she needed to be talked to. She needed to be asked easy questions, questions that let her choose between answering, "I've been driving so many dance carpools that I feel like a taxi driver," or "I had a rough chemo session this week and my eyebrows fell out."

She understood that she needed to choose, more often than not, to feel cared for when people bumbled conversations around her and said the wrong thing.

With each passing day, the Father was helping her to know her own self, and to trust him more.

She chose truthful words for Eleanor now. "This week has been a good one. But there've been bad ones too. I've been scared, and I've been discouraged. And I've spent the past days rejoicing that, for however long it lasts, I'm so lucky to be Joe's wife, and Kate and Heidi's mother." She reached for a pottery dish filled with sweet potatoes that someone had brought. "You see this? This pottery had to be formed and fired, painted and re-fired, for it to turn out as beautiful and colorful and *useful* as it is now. There are days when I feel like that's where I am, Eleanor. In the fire, burning up. That's when I have to remind myself that the kiln is making me into some useful new vessel for the Lord."

Eleanor squeezed her hand. "Your friends are here for you, to help you walk through this. We may not do it right, but we want you to let us try."

"Thank you." Theia hugged her. "I need to let you do that. For so long, I've tried not to let anybody know that I was afraid. And I've been so alone."

The buzzer on the stove went off. Joe came into the kitchen with a troop of men brandishing knives.

"Now that's a scary sight, all those armed men in the kitchen."

"Out, out, all of you!" Theia grinned at Eleanor, rose from the chair, and shooed the men out of the kitchen with her apron like she'd shoo a flock of geese. "Eleanor has to take care of the stuffing first. Then we'll call you."

"We can just cut into it, can't we? The stuffing will fall out."

"Women have a way that they like to do things, and that isn't it."

Between the two genders, the great crowd of people managed to get everything uncovered and cut to serve, ice in glasses, tea poured, dressing in a bowl with a silver serving spoon, and a mountain of turkey sliced to perfection. Everyone oohed and aahed when Joe set the huge platter of meat on the table before them.

Winston Taylor volunteered to eat one of the legs whole.

Jaycee's little brothers began to shout at top volume for the wishbone.

Theia joined hands with Eleanor on her right and Sarah on her left. From across the way, her husband winked at her and mouthed, "I love you." They had prayed together and had decided on the order of things just this morning.

Joe began. "Before we thank the Lord for the meal, Theia has something she wants to say to everybody here."

Lord, even while I walk through darkness, shine your light through me.

"We invited you all here because we love you. Because the Lord loves you, too, and he's put you in our lives now, at a time when we need you the most." Her voice faltered. "We have not been easy to stand beside these past few months, but you have done it anyway. On this day of all days, when we offer up thanksgiving to our Father, we want to tell you that we thank God for you. We thank him for your work produced by faith, your labor prompted by love, and your endurance inspired by hope in our Lord Jesus Christ."

Down the table, Jaycee's mother Lois picked up the index card that had been propped beside her goblet. Jaycee had told her mother about the Lord and had invited her several times to come to church but, so far, she hadn't. "Can I read this?" she asked, her voice almost as shaky as Theia's. "I don't read the Bible much, but I'd like to read it today."

Theia nodded. "Oh, Lois. Please do."

"Come, let us sing for joy to the Lord; let us shout aloud to the Rock, of our salvation. Let us come before him with thanksgiving and extol him with music and song."

Lois's gentle, hope-filled voice encircled the table even as they all encircled it with their clasped hands.

Joe prayed after that, and everyone started talking and passing the feast.

Theia hadn't been able to get back into her own kitchen all afternoon.

Kate, Heidi, and Jaycee had made quick work of cleaning up and filling the dishwasher. Others had served coffee and wrapped up the leftovers and left plates out with treats for everyone to nibble while they watched football. Theia had even taken a nap.

It wasn't until almost dusk, after everyone had gone home and she went in to make a pot of tea, that she found the package wrapped in ancient tissue paper and tied with twine.

"What's this?" she asked anyone within earshot.

"Something your dad brought over when he came in this morning. I don't know."

She untied the string, tore open the paper.

When she recognized it, her hands started to tremble. She couldn't swallow past the lump in her throat.

"Joe, this is my mother's Bible."

"How can that be?"

"I don't know. Dad must have found it somewhere."

Theia set her teacup down in the precise center of the saucer. She lifted the large, worn leather book from its wrappings, and the pages fell open. Pencil notes, gleaned from Edna's favorite sermons and studies, lined the margins. In almost every chapter, verses had been underlined, and some of them even dated.

"All of her notes are here. All of the things she was learning when she—"

Joe came up behind her and captured her shoulders. "—when she got cancer?"

Theia nodded. "And before."

Her hands drifted to the brittle yellowed pages, fingering them as if they were gold. Out the window she could see the light in her father's greenhouse, his dark silhouette stooped over the gardener's bench.

"I've got to talk to him," she said to Joe.

Harry glanced up when she knocked on the screen. "Anybody home?"

He raised a trowel in her direction and gestured for her to enter. "That was a fine meal today, Theia. A fine meal." The light from the bulb above him seemed to catch in his eyes and gleam there.

She went inside, taking a deep breath of the smells of her father, of old fabric and of loose, dark soil in the greenhouse, of potash and bone meal and nitrogen and of new warm things growing outdoors. She held the Bible in her hands.

"I found it, Daddy. Thank you."

He drove the trowel deep into the dirt. "Thought you could put that to good use right about now."

"I thought her Bible had gotten thrown out with the rest of her things. It's been missing for years."

He turned to her then and quietly told her the story of how he'd sealed it away in the box.

"The more I kept praying for you, Theia, the more I kept thinking about that box. I swept your mother's life away before I'd scarcely even given you the chance to grieve for her. It was the wrong thing to do."

Theia moved over to lay her head against the rough flannel of her father's work shirt. Whenever they touched one another, it became suddenly difficult to discern who was holding whom for comfort. Her own father seemed so much smaller, so much more feeble, than she'd even noticed before. As if he were withering away somehow. As if she'd become the parent and he the child. "It's okay. You didn't know."

"Should have learned a long time ago that, when you try to push aside the difficult things that happen in people's lives, you are also pushing aside God's power to heal and reconstruct."

"Maybe that's what he's doing now. Giving us both a second chance for healing." They released each other and stepped back, eyes locked for a long moment.

Harry turned back to the trowel. He selected a begonia from a plastic flat, turned it upside down and emptied the squared soil and root into his gnarled old hands. "There's more inside that Bible than you've found."

"What do you mean, Dad?"

"Just look."

She began to thumb through the pages. "There's notes in here. And a church bulletin from some service back in 1979."

"Keep looking."

For a while Theia did not see the envelope. But the page fell open and she recognized the scalloped edge, the tiny pink roses, sky-blue paper as thin as an autumn-cured leaf. She picked it up, an odd lost expression in her eyes. "What's this?"

"Maybe you can tell me."

She flipped the envelope over and saw her name written there in her mother's strong, slanted script.

Theia ran her fingernail under the flap and, with the greatest of care, opened a letter from her mother that had been sealed away for twenty-two years.

Dearest Theia,

If you are reading this letter now, it means that I have gone home to be with the Father, and you are looking through my Bible.

It is the most difficult thing I have ever done, thinking of leaving you and your father behind. But leave you behind, I must. I have faith in God and I have faith in the two of you. I know that, after I leave, you and your father will make it just fine. But you're going to have to help him a little bit. He's going to be lonely for a while, until he gets used to being without me.

I remind you now, and someday you will know, that healing isn't always what others think it is. They think to be healed is to be cured of something. But to be healed is to be made whole. And I have been made whole, even though my body is against me, because cancer has made me realize that Jesus is here with me, loving me, telling me secret things about myself, holding my heart. This has been, because of that new discovery, the most glorious time of my life.

You, my precious daughter, are the one who has prayed the most that I might be healed. As I go, I stand firm on the belief that God

114

does not cause cancer in the world. When you are older, you will understand. Prayer for healing must be, in the end, as in everything else, the perfect act of trusting God. Isn't relinquishment of everything to God very much the same as acceptance that God is in everything?

You grew up so fast, my daughter. You haven't worn these ribbons in your hair in a long time. I found them on the shelf beside my hairbrush today and thought you might enjoy having them to remember our mornings by.

I will miss you, and I entrust you into the Father's perfect care.

All my love,

Mama

Two blue satin hair ribbons fell out of the folds of the letter, making two perfect curls in the flat of Theia's hand.

Theia held the strands of blue satin ribbon up for her father to see. They represented so much to her. A childhood that she had almost let herself lose because parts of it were painful to remember. A loving mother who had done her best to teach her to grow and walk in courage and in freedom, despite the obstacle of an incurable disease.

Harry hoisted his latest potted begonia high on the shelf. "Anything in that letter that an old man might get to hear about?"

"Plenty." Theia laid her head in a careful place, against the broad of his back where he still seemed strong and young, where she could feel his heart beating. "She had faith in us, Dad. She knew we'd be okay."

He turned and she could see the tears in her father's eyes. "A good woman, my Edna," he said with a sad, wise smile. "Guess it's time I stopped thinking about why she died. Guess it's time I started thinking about why she lived. She lived for us, Theia. She lived for us and she lived for her Lord. Just the way you're doing now with your husband and your girls."

For a moment, Theia stared at the ribbons, winding them between her fingers the same way she had wound Kate's hair not so long ago. Then she reached behind the nape of her neck and, with no further ado, tied them into a double bow at the base of her throat. There would be no more ponytails or plaits for a while, not until her hair grew back.

"Mama used to call these my magic hair ribbons, remember? She started it the first day of school, when I was afraid to go.

"I'm scared," I would whisper as Mama sent me out the door with a new satchel packed full of Elmer's glue and tissues, map pencils and a ruler. 'What if my new teacher doesn't like me? What if I get on the wrong bus? What if I have to sit by Larry Wells?'

"'I'll tell you what,' and Mama would wink as she tied a bow on one of my braids. 'Whenever you feel afraid of something, we'll just tie these into your hair. They will remind you that I'm praying for you. That I'm right beside you. That God is right beside you. That way you won't have to worry anymore, about anything.'"

She was quiet for a while, remembering the afternoon Larry Wells threatened to steal her lunch box, the Friday-afternoon spelling tests, the fifth-grade choir concert when she'd had to sing 'Fifty Nifty' by herself onstage. By that time, she'd been so old she'd insisted on wearing the ribbons not in her hair but tied to her shoe.

"If any fear lingered," she told Harry, "I went through the whole day reminding myself that Mom had put those ribbons in my hair."

The same way she was learning to get through each day with cancer, reminding herself of God's presence in her life.

Harry took another tin bucket off the shelf and drove a nail in the bottom with one easy *thwack*. He turned it right side up and started to place rocks inside. "Remember how Edna used to stuff her

Thanksgiving turkeys? Remember how she used to stand it upside down in the sink and wiggle its legs and tell us it was doing the tango so it wouldn't go down the drain?"

Theia tucked her mother's letter back inside the Bible, ready to carry it back to her home. "Oh, Daddy." She kissed him on the sandpapery cheek. "How could I ever forget?"

Opening night of *The Nutcracker* pandemonium reigned backstage at The Pink Garter Theater.

"My wing is torn." One of the littlest angels tugged on Theia's sweater. "Can you sew it for me?"

"I can't find my leotard." A reindeer jingled her bell harness for attention.

"The Sugar Plum Fairy can't find her crown."

When Julie Stevens had asked if she'd volunteer for the dance program, Theia had in mind something quiet like ushering or taking tickets. But the concert committee obviously had something else in mind. So here she stood, trying to figure out how to clean the grape juice out of Dillon Mason's jabot before he had to dance in the party scene, dabbing circles of Shangri-La Ruby lipstick on each reindeer's nose, and making certain that no one chewed gum when they lined up to take the stage.

Ten minutes before the show began, Julie Stevens came behind the curtain and crouched close to her dancers. They gathered around her as she gave them last-minute encouragement and suggestions. "We've got a full house out there tonight, so be sure to dance your best. Angels, when you make the arch with your scepters remember to make a slow big motion, big enough to carry to the last row of the theater."

Eight angels nodded, their halos bobbing.

"Mice, when you throw the cannonballs, remember that they are heavy. *Heavy.* You are not throwing plastic balls around. You are battling, iron against iron."

One mouse flexed her forearm, proudly showing everyone some muscle.

"Reindeer. I don't care what else happens out there. Do *not* get too far ahead of the sleigh."

"We won't," they all shrieked while jingling the bells on their harnesses one more time.

"Sh-hh-hh, now, everyone. This is it. What we've been working toward for months. I'm on my way to the sound booth."

The dance students cheered.

Just as Julie Stevens headed downstage, she and Heidi McKinnis almost collided. "Have a good time out there tonight, Heidi. You've worked really hard, and I know it. I'm proud of you, learning the new dance the way you have." The two women locked eyes over Heidi's head. "I'm glad you're here tonight, Mrs. McKinnis."

Theia inclined her jaw. "I am, too." That's all that needed to be said.

In the theater the overture swelled and, on stage, the spotlights faded from twilight to black. They came up again in lavish colors of blue, green, red, yellow, bathing the set, an English Victorian parlor decorated for a party, and the Christmas tree in radiant light. Party-goers, young and old, began dancing their way up the aisles toward the stage.

"Even though you're working back here, are you going to go out in the audience and see me dance?" Heidi whispered.

Theia nodded. "I wouldn't miss it. They said I could sneak out and sit on the stairs to watch."

"Where are Grandpa and Dad and Kate?"

Theia opened the side of the curtain just an inch. "Over there." She pointed. "See. On the fourth row."

There they were, all three of them, their faces captured in the vivid lighting. Theia closed the curtain. Heidi nodded at the double bow Theia had pinned to the chest of her sweater. "You wear those ribbons Grandma gave you all the time now, don't you?"

"Yes, I do. I brought them along for a special reason tonight, though. Just in case you thought you might want to borrow them."

Heidi checked her braids, pinned with what felt like six hundred bobby pins and sprayed with hair lacquer so they wouldn't give way during the cartwheels. "There isn't any place to put them."

"If you wanted, we could always come up with something."

"I *have* been a little afraid all afternoon. What if I mess up the cartwheels after I've practiced them so many times?"

"Remember what I taught you. It's all in the rhythm. *Hand. Hand. Foot. Foot.*"

"Can you tie them on my arm, Mom? That way I'll know they're there, but no one else can see them."

"Ah. There you go. Perfect idea." She unpinned the ribbons from her sweater and made a lovely bow on her daughter's arm with a flourish. "I'll be praying that every cartwheel lands just right."

Heidi pulled her sleeve down over them.

"Clowns. Three minutes! Line up."

"That's you. You're on."

Heidi took a deep breath, smoothed her pantaloons and lifted her chin. "I'm ready."

Theia kissed her good-bye, snuck past the curtain, and found a place on the steps so she could watch. Minutes passed. The stage stayed bright. Suddenly, music surged again through the theater. Mother Ginger clumped across the stage on her stilts, hid a giggle behind her gloved hand and lifted her swaying skirts. Out cart wheeled five clowns. *Hand. Hand. Foot. Foot.* Each of them landed perfectly. Heidi tilted her beaming face up toward the lights, and began to dance.

Another Kind of Sanctuary

By the time Mrs. Halley finished telling her story and returned the blue ribbon to the jar, Beth had an enormous lump in her throat and her eyes were swimming with tears.

"My goodness," the pastor's widow said, looking at her watch. "I didn't mean to go on so long. I've interrupted your work. You must think me a bother." She started to rise.

"No!" Beth said quickly. "Please don't go yet. I—I don't have that much more to do."

"Well, if you're sure you don't mind, I'm in no hurry to leave. This church has been a part of my life for twelve years. It's difficult to say farewell." She sat back in the pew again. "Enough about me. Why don't you tell me about you and your boys? You said you have two sons?"

"Yes. Tommy's nineteen and Mark is seventeen. Nearly grown. But if they keep going in the direction they're headed now, I don't know what will . . ." With a shake of her head, Beth's sentence faded into silence.

She was at her wits' end, completely out of answers, and she didn't think she wanted to air her problems to a stranger, no matter how kind Mrs. Halley was.

Mrs. Halley seemed to understand. "It's always a challenge, being a parent. Every stage of their lives brings new dilemmas with it. But children *are* a blessing from the Lord. Of that I'm sure."

Did teenagers count as children? Or as alien beings?

Mrs. Halley held out the jar. "Could I trouble you to use your glass cleaner on this? It's gotten rather dusty there underneath the chair for who knows how long."

"Sure." Beth took the jar and set it on the floor, then pulled a cloth and a spray bottle from the pail of cleaning supplies.

"I wonder what John would want me to do with it."

"Take it with you to Florida, I imagine. Sounds like you're the only one who'd know all the stories that go with the things inside."

"Oh, I do! I know so many of them! And they should always be shared. It's such fun to see all of these things again."

Beth reached in to pull out an old skeleton key.

"What about this one?"

"Oh mercy, yes! That belonged to Grace Riverton. She and her husband had six children and a small house. A very small house. But it was a house filled with love. No doubt about it. Still, it was crowded, and sometimes Grace complained about not having any space of her own." Mrs. Halley laughed softly. "So those kids got together and decided to build a tree house where she could go when she wanted to get away from them."

"A tree house?"

"A tree house. Goodness knows where they collected all the wood and other materials, but collect it they did. And when it was done, they hung a beat-up old door so she could lock the whole world out." Mrs. Halley held up the key. "When Grace dropped this in the story jar, she said she'd learned that shutting out the

122

world was the last thing she wanted to do when the world was where her kids were."

Beth shifted her weight from her left hip to her right. "Are you tired? Will you tell another story from the jar?"

"Oh, here's one that's interesting." After wiping the mouth of the jar clean, Mrs. Halley reached inside and pulled out a purple-heart medal.

"Who brought that?"

"This belonged to Nora Weaver. Her late husband was awarded this purple-heart when he was injured during Desert Storm. Nora actually placed this in the jar just last year when her youngest son Tommy was sent to Afghanistan."

"I don't know how any mother can stand to see her child sent to be in harm's way." Beth shook her head. "I can't imagine how hard that would be."

"I can't imagine it, either." Mrs. Halley said. "Nora told us that one morning just before dawn, her eyes flew open and she couldn't sleep. She knew her son must need prayer that instant. Nora stood from her bed and fell to her knees. 'Lord, hold Tommy in the palm of your hand,' she prayed. 'Whatever it is that you've called our boy to do, give him the strength to carry it through. No matter what it is.'"

"W-what happened?" Beth was almost afraid to ask.

"When Nora dropped this in the story jar, she told us how she'd waited for days to hear some word from her youngest son. She didn't know whether Tommy was alive or dead. Then the e-mail came. Tommy's note was so excited that he almost couldn't get the words typed. About noon, the very day, the very minute Nora had felt called to pray, their armored vehicle passed a little girl crying in the street. Tommy wanted to stop and help her. The others in the convoy argued that it was too dangerous."

"I'm sure it *was* dangerous," Beth said. "Did they stop?"

"They did. Tommy argued until they let him out. He spoke to the girl and gave her a lollipop. He held her hand and told her everything would be okay."

"And that was that?"

"Yes. That was that," Mrs. Halley said pointedly, "except for the roadside bomb that detonated three minutes later, in exactly the place they would have been if they hadn't listened to Tommy. The little girl and Tommy's lollipop saved at least a dozen lives that day."

Beth sat mesmerized. Did everything in this jar have such significance behind it? Did every story have an ending that hinted at a mother's miracle?

"Do you see that cat's eye?" Mrs. Halley pointed. "I dropped that marble in the story jar myself when our son was five years old. It was a reminder to take time to play. Life doesn't always have to be serious. God means for us to have fun, too. To laugh and play games. So I learned to play marbles with our son and kept at it even after he grew up and moved halfway across the country."

"What about this one?" Beth pointed at the small curl of a seashell she could see inside the jar.

"Ah, yes. The seashell." Mrs. Halley shifted in her chair as she spoke. "Sue Jackson put this in after she and her two kids spent a day along the beach. She told how they'd been walking along, marveling at the differences in shape and size of their footprints. She told how they'd laughed at the cold, wet sand as it squished between their toes. They squealed as the waves slid toward them and dashed over their ankles. That's when the beauty of God's creation overwhelmed Sue. Everywhere she looked, she couldn't get away from his presence. The power of the sea as it rolled onto shore reminded her of the power of God's word. The perfection of the little hands clasped inside her own reminded her of God's attention to every detail in her life."

"It seems like, well, that God stories can be very complicated," Beth commented. "Other times they can be so simple."

"Yes. They can." Mrs. Halley peered into the container again. "You picked out the last one, Beth. Why don't you select another?"

Beth reached into the jar, smiling. After surveying several other objects, she pulled out a small, delicate silver earring from the jar. "What about this one? Does it have a match? Do you know its story?"

"Oh my, yes. Leah Carpenter came forward to share her joy on a very special Mother's Day. Hmmm. I guess that must have been in the jar for a good long time. These rings are much more a simple fashion statement now than they used to be in the 1980's. Back when Leah told us her story, a girl who wore one of these wasn't looked on too kindly. The nose ring you're holding belonged to Leah's daughter, Shoshanna."

"It's a *nose* ring?" Beth felt her eyes widen as she looked at the silver hoop again. Maybe things were different today than they'd been back then. But Beth still thought piercings and tattoos were kind of tacky. She recognized the type of people who wore body jewelry. She'd seen them hanging around the high school whenever she'd had to visit the principal regarding one of her boys. She thought she might be stereotyping people, but she didn't like kids who dressed Goth. She saw them as hoodlums and troublemakers, the whole group of them.

How does something like this represent one of God's miracles? She held it up to give it a better inspection.

Mrs. Halley seemed to read her thoughts. "You never know what the good Lord will use to draw a person unto himself. He works in mysterious ways, his wonders to perform. Leah and Shoshanna were certainly evidence of that."

"I think I'd like to hear this story," Beth said, doubtful but curious.

"And I'd love to share it with you." Mrs. Halley chuckled softly as she settled deeper into the wing chair. "It all began when Shoshanna was sixteen years old. . . ."

Part Two

HEART RINGS

by

ROBIN LEE HATCHER

To my daughter, Jennifer Lee.

One of God's greatest gifts to me is you.
You taught me so much about looking
beneath the surface and into the heart.
Thanks for the creative license
you've granted with this story.

Love, Mom

*"The LORD doesn't make decisions the way you do!
People judge by outward appearance, but the LORD
looks at a person's thoughts and intentions."*
(1 Samuel 16:7b NLB)

Lost and Found

Seated at the head table overlooking the banquet hall, Leah Carpenter fought to keep her anger in check.

"Relax, honey," Wes whispered near her ear. "Give her some time. Traffic's bad out there tonight. Shoshanna will get here. She promised."

Leah glanced at the empty chair below the podium, then at her husband. "She's doing this to spite me."

He shook his head and discreetly caught her hand below the tablecloth, sadness in his eyes.

She was thankful he didn't argue with her. Not tonight. Not this night of all nights.

How many women had been honored by the town of Beaker Heights as Citizen of the Year? None. Leah was the first.

She'd been selected for this honor because of Together We Can, a non-profit organization that helped homeless women, especially single mothers, get on their feet and back into the work force. In the years since it was founded, Together We Can—Leah's brain-child—had become a model for similar community programs around the country.

Leah had given countless hours to make certain her labor of love succeeded. She'd poured herself into it, giving a hundred and ten percent. There were times, especially in the beginning, when others on the non-profit corporation's board of directors wanted to give up, but she'd talk it up again, convince them to hang in there. She was talking to herself too.

Tonight, the people of Beaker Heights were recognizing her accomplishments.

And her daughter wouldn't be there to see it.

Why am I surprised? I should have known she'd do this.

She'd had a dreadful argument with Shoshanna last night. Their sixteen-year-old daughter had announced she wanted to get her nose pierced, like her friend Krissie Jenkins. Leah had gone over the top at the very suggestion, grounding Shoshanna for a week and forbidding her to see Krissie.

A pierced nose? No child of Leah Carpenter's was going to do such a thing. What would people think if she allowed her daughter to parade around town with a ring in her nose? She didn't care if body piercings were almost common among young folk these days. It was an act of rebellion, and she'd seen firsthand where such rebellion led. Just look at the women Together We Can was helping.

It wasn't much comfort when Wes suggested she was overreacting. "She's sixteen, for crying out loud," he'd said after Shoshanna fled the room in tears. "She's *supposed* to push the boundaries. It's part of growing up."

He's always been too easy on her, Leah thought now, her resentment increasing. *I have to play the heavy, and he gets to be the favorite adult. It isn't fair.*

She picked up her fork and moved the food around on her plate without taking a bite. Reluctantly she finally admitted she wasn't being fair to Wes, her husband of three years. When he entered her life, he'd filled a place in her heart that she'd thought could never be filled after twelve years as a widow. He was good to her in countless ways, and he loved Shoshanna as if she were his own daughter. The feeling was mutual, too, so much so that Shoshanna had legally changed her name to Carpenter last year.

Leah glanced at Wes. When their gazes met, she gave him a tiny smile. In return, he reached again for her hand beneath the table.

Maybe I did overreact. Maybe forbidding Shoshanna to see Krissie was a bit harsh.

Wes's grip on her hand tightened. "Look who's here."

She turned and saw Shoshanna being escorted to her table. She felt a rush of relief. Thank goodness. Tonight meant so much to Leah, and if her daughter hadn't come to share it with—

Her thoughts died as the small silver ring in Shoshanna's left nostril glittered in the light of the crystal chandeliers.

Something twisted in Leah's chest.

Something painful.

Her baby. Her beautiful, loving, sunshine girl. Her precious child—who for the better part of her sixteen years had brought her mother nothing but joy—had defied Leah's wishes and had her nose pierced.

No matter what happened next, the evening was ruined.

. . . .

"How could you do it?" Leah stood in the doorway to Shoshanna's basement bedroom. "How could you embarrass me in front of all those people? Did you see the way they looked at you?"

"There's no reason for you to be embarrassed, Mom. *I'm* the one with the nose ring. Besides, it's no big deal."

"It's a big deal to me. Good heavens! Don't you realize how you look? Don't you know what people think of kids who mutilate their bodies like this? They'll think—they'll think you're on drugs."

Shoshanna flicked a strand of long blonde hair over her shoulder. "You know what your problem is, Mom? You're always worried about what other people think. What about what *I* think? Doesn't that count for anything in this family? I think this ring is cool. I like it. Besides, it isn't any different than an earring, you know."

"It *is* different, and you will remove that hideous piece of metal from your face. I won't allow a daughter of mine to have a pierced nose!"

"But, Mom, I—"

"Tonight," she interrupted, her voice rising even higher. Leah clenched her hands into tight fists at her side. "Do you hear me, Shoshanna Marie Carpenter? When I see you in the morning, that . . . *thing* . . . will be gone. We'll discuss your punishment then."

She turned and strode from the room, wincing when she heard the door slam behind her.

Wes was waiting for her in their second-story bedroom. "How'd it go?"

She gave her head a slight shake, then went into the walk-in closet and began to get ready for bed.

Her husband appeared in the doorway. "Leah?"

"I told her she had to remove that—that ugly thing from her face." She draped her tailored suit jacket over a padded hanger. "I told her we would discuss punishment in the morning."

Wes was silent for a few moments before saying, "She loves you, honey. Try to remember that."

"Well, this is a fine way to show it." With her back toward him, she closed her eyes against an unwelcome urge to cry.

"Didn't you ever rebel as a teen?"

"Not like this." She swallowed the lump in her throat. "How can you defend her? If it was up to you, I suppose she could do anything she pleased."

His hand alighted on her shoulder, and he gently turned her to face him. "I'm not saying what she did was right or that she shouldn't receive appropriate punishment for her disobedience. I'm just suggesting that you think carefully about what you do or say next."

Unable to reply, she turned away. Anger, disappointment, frustration, and a host of indefinable emotions roiled inside her.

When does it get easier?

Surely she'd had enough turmoil in her life. She'd been widowed while still in her twenties. She'd raised her daughter alone. She'd scrimped and saved and struggled to get by and given up many things so Shoshanna wouldn't feel deprived. Why did her once-perfect child have to turn against her like this? After all she'd done. After all she'd given.

It wasn't fair.

Wes had moved up behind her, and she felt his arms slide around her. It felt nice. If only she could let him handle this. She was tired of being strong.

But she couldn't. Shoshanna was her daughter and her responsibility. She would have to decide on the punishment and then see it through.

"She's a good kid," Wes said softly. "You've raised her right. She'll come through this. What's the Bible say? 'Raise up a child in the way she should go, and when she's grown, she won't depart from it.'"

"Oh, Wes." She stepped out of his embrace. "That's no help. Not now. I need *real* answers."

He shrugged. "Some folks think God's word *is* a real answer, Leah."

She sighed as she turned away to unzip her skirt. The tension in her shoulders made her want to scream. She knew Wes wanted to talk more about it. But finally she heard him leave the walk-in.

She felt a sting of guilt. It wasn't that she didn't believe the Bible was God's Word, although she knew that was how it had sounded to Wes. At one time, she'd found comfort when reading the Scriptures, something she hadn't found time for in ages.

She shook off the thought and her guilt. Right now she needed to find a solution to her problem. She hadn't the patience to wait upon God to see what he would say. She had to have an answer tonight.

But it wouldn't matter what solution she arrived at.

By morning Shoshanna was gone.

A New Page

Two years later ...

Cindy Markowitz leaned through the open doorway of Leah's office. "Did you hear the news? Dwayne's wife had her baby last night. A little girl. Everybody's doing fine."

"Oh, that's wonderful." Leah forced a smile, ignoring the sudden ache in her chest. "They did so want a daughter this time."

"A bunch of us are going over to the hospital at noon. Want to come along?"

"Sorry. I can't today. I've got a lunch date with Wes. But give Patricia my love and tell her I'll come to see her soon."

"I'll do it. Say hi to Wes for me." Cindy disappeared from view.

Pressing her lips together, Leah rose from her chair, walked to the door, and closed it.

She could have told Dwayne and Patricia Jones that they might very well be sorry some day, that they might wish they'd stopped having children after the birth of their third son, that a daughter could bring them more joy and more sorrow than they imagined possible.

When does the pain go away?

She leaned her back against the door and closed her eyes, fighting tears.

If only I could know where she is. If only I knew she's okay, that she's safe, if she's healthy, if she's got food to eat.

Leah had received two phone calls from Shoshanna, both within the first six months after her sudden departure from home. Both calls ended badly, with Leah saying things she later regretted and with Shoshanna obviously hanging up in anger.

"Oh, baby girl," Leah whispered. "I'm so sorry. I'm so very sorry."

Drawing a deep breath, she straightened her shoulders and returned to her desk. She wasn't going to sink into those maudlin spirits again. She'd done far too much of that in the past two years. She recognized all the symptoms. She also knew it had far more to do with the recent date of Shoshanna's birthday than with the arrival of the Jones baby.

She's eighteen now.

A knot formed in Leah's belly.

If she's alive.

A shudder ran through her, as it always did when that horrendous possibility sprang into her mind.

Please, God, let her be alive.

The phone rang, startling Leah.

"Hi, hon," Wes said when she answered. "About lunch—"

"Don't tell me it's noon already." She glanced at the wall clock.

"No, but I need to cancel our lunch date. I have to meet with . . . someone from out of town. Noon seems to be the only time available. Can we reschedule for tomorrow?"

Well, it was probably for the best. Wes would know the moment he saw her that she was having one of her blue days. It made him feel helpless when she got like this. He wanted to fix it, make it better, and he couldn't.

"That okay, hon?" he asked.

"Sure. Tomorrow's good for me. It's better if I stay in the office today anyway. You should see the stack of papers on my desk, and I've got a newspaper reporter coming for an interview at three this afternoon. I haven't begun to prepare for that yet."

"Want me to bring home Chinese for supper? Fried rice? Sweet and sour pork? Egg rolls?"

"My hero," she said with a sigh, meaning it.

He chuckled. "I take it that means all of the above."

"Yes, please."

"Leah?"

"Hmm?"

"I love you."

"I love you, too."

"See you around 5:30."

"Okay. 'Bye."

"'Bye."

She placed the handset in its cradle, wondering as she stared at the phone how she would have made it through the past two years without Wes to lean on.

The answer was simple: She wouldn't have.

It was pouring down rain by the time Leah left the Together We Can offices on Main Street. Visibility was low, and traffic snarled its way through the Beaker Heights business district. Leah muttered more than one uncharitable word at fellow drivers as she inched her way out of the downtown core. It seemed an eternity before she reached the freeway.

When she arrived home forty minutes later, she was surprised to discover Wes's 1965 Ford Mustang already parked in the garage. She couldn't imagine how he'd managed to pick up dinner and beat her home. Not with traffic as bad as it was tonight.

She pulled into her space in the garage, cut the engine, reached for her purse and leather briefcase. As she got out of the car, her stomach growled, reminding her that she'd worked through lunch. Chinese take-out was sounding better and better.

Maybe they should eat by candlelight in the family room. She could light a fire in the fireplace and put on one of Wes's favorite soundtracks. A romantic evening with her husband might be just the ticket to improve her doldrums. Besides, it wouldn't hurt to remind Wes how much she loved and appreciated him.

She opened the door into the house. "I'm home," she called.

She sniffed the air expectantly. Not even a whiff of sweet and sour pork.

"Wes?"

He appeared in the kitchen doorway. "I was starting to get worried." He glanced over his shoulder, then back at Leah. "I tried to call you at the office, but you'd already left."

"Traffic was a bear. How'd you miss it?"

"I . . . ah . . . Well, the truth is I didn't go back to the office this afternoon."

She looked at him more closely. He had something serious to tell her. She could see it in his eyes. "Why not?"

"Maybe you ought to sit down."

A shiver of alarm swept through her. "Tell me what it is."

From the kitchen came a soft voice, "It's me, Mom."

Leah did sit then. Not by choice but because her knees buckled beneath her. She sank onto the edge of the sofa, barely keeping from sliding off onto the floor.

"Sho?" she said, but no sound came out of her mouth.

Wes strode forward, his expression anxious. He knelt on one knee in front of Leah and took both of her hands between his, squeezing gently. For a moment, he seemed to plead with her with his eyes. Then a movement at the edge of her vision drew Leah's gaze from her husband toward the kitchen doorway.

It was Shoshanna—a very different girl from the daughter in the photographs Leah had stared at every day for the past two years. She looked taller and thinner than when she'd left home. Her face had matured as had her figure. She wore tight-fitting, faded jeans with a hole in one knee, a bulky blue sweater, a leather jacket, and what looked like army boots. She also wore a small ring in her nose.

But it wasn't her clothes or her looks or even that offensive piece of jewelry that stopped Leah's breathing. It was something worse.

Shoshanna was all but bald. Her beautiful blonde hair, gone, her scalp covered by little more than peach fuzz. She resembled the photos of people after chemotherapy and radiation.

Oh please, no!

"Hi, Mom." The wraith of a girl moved slowly into the living room.

Pressing a fist to the base of her throat, Leah rose to her feet. "Wes—Dad met you?"

"Yeah. I . . . I didn't know if you'd want to see me after the things I said to you. I thought I'd better check with Dad first."

"Oh, Sho. How could you believe I wouldn't want to see you? Even for a moment? I've been so worried." She steeled herself for the bad news. "Tell me what's wrong."

"Wrong?" Shoshanna glanced toward her stepfather, then back at Leah. "Nothing's wrong. Everything's great now. It's why I came back."

"You needn't pretend for my sake." Leah blinked away her tears. "I want the truth. What have the doctors told you?"

"What doctors?"

"Beaker Heights has one of the best research hospitals in the country. I'm sure they—"

"Mom, what're you talking about? I don't need a hospital or any doctors." Shoshanna smiled. "I'm fine. Healthy as a horse, as Grandma used to say."

"But . . . but your hair. It's gone. I thought . . . I was afraid . . ." She let her words fade into silence, confused.

Her daughter's eyes widened a fraction—and then she laughed. "I'm not sick, Mom. I just shaved my head."

"Whatever for?"

"Well . . ." Shoshanna's amused smile vanished. "I guess now's as good a time as any." She drew a deep breath before turning her head, offering Leah a profile. "I shaved it so people could see my tattoo."

Her tattoo?

Wes placed an arm around Leah's shoulders. Perhaps he feared she would pass out. Or worse, say something she couldn't ever take back.

Through the half-inch of pale-gold hair that covered Shoshanna's scalp, Leah saw what appeared to be a large falling star, streaking across the right side of her daughter's head.

She couldn't think of anything to say. Not one single word. Her mind was a complete blank.

"It started out as a joke," Shoshanna said softly, turning to face her mother again.

"A—a *joke*?"

Her daughter nodded. "And you might as well know. I've got another one."

"Another one?"

"Uh huh." Shoshanna touched her right shoulder blade with her left hand. "Back here. Of the earth."

How was Leah supposed to respond? She didn't know what was expected of her, what was the right thing to say, the right way to react. If she said the wrong thing, Shoshanna might leave again, and Leah couldn't bear that. She couldn't.

But a tattoo?

Two of them?

"Mom . . ."

Leah felt as if something were crushing her heart.

"Mom, I need to tell you I'm sorry."

She met her daughter's gaze.

"I'm sorry I ran away and caused you to worry about me all this time. I'm sorry I didn't let you know I was okay. I should've let you know I loved you and missed you. I *did* miss you, something awful. And I'm sorry I disobeyed you so much when I *was* at home." Tears slipped down Shoshanna's cheeks. "I'd like to come home, for at least a while, if you'll let me. I'd understand if you don't. Really I will. But I hope you'll be able to forgive me and let me come home. I'd like to see if we can't make things right between us."

Wes gave Leah a light squeeze of encouragement.

"Things'll be different than before, Mom. I promise."

Tearfully, Leah gathered her daughter into her arms, still unable to speak for the lump in her throat.

Please, God, let it all be different than before.

Dress for Success

Still sleepless at four in the morning, Leah rose from the bed, slipped on her robe, and knotted the belt around her waist. On her way to the kitchen, she paused in the hall to bump up the thermostat. A short while later, the coffee was perking and the furnace was pouring heat through the vents.

Not that she paid any attention as she stood before the sliding glass door, staring into the darkness beyond, her arms crossed over her chest.

"What did I do that was so wrong?" she whispered to the glass.

She'd been a good mother. She'd given Shoshanna everything she could. Whatever her daughter had been interested in, she'd involved herself in also. When Shoshanna wanted to be a Girl Scout, Leah had become a Girl Scout leader. When Shoshanna wanted to be a ballerina, Leah had watched her practice and attended every performance. She had read to her daughter and held her when she hurt and explained the facts of life in gentle but clear terms. She had laughed with Shoshanna and cried with Shoshanna. Right up until Shoshanna's sixteenth year, they'd been close. Closer than most mothers and daughters. At least she'd thought so.

"Mom?"

With a little start, Leah turned from the window. "You surprised me."

"Sorry." Standing in the kitchen doorway, Shoshanna ran the fingers of one hand over the fuzz on her head while squinting at Leah with sleepy eyes. "What're you doing up at this hour?"

"Making coffee. It's ready. Do you want some?"

"Sure. I guess." Shoshanna yawned as she shuffled toward the kitchen table. "It's still raining. Never let up all night. I could hear it running through the gutters."

Leah crossed the kitchen and took two mugs from the cupboard. She filled them with coffee from the carafe, then carried them to the table, setting one down in front of Shoshanna.

"Got any cream, Mom? If not, milk'll do fine."

Strange, the way Shoshanna's request upset Leah. A mother should know that her daughter liked cream in her coffee.

Shoshanna didn't wait for a reply. She rose from her chair and walked to the refrigerator. With her head hidden from view as she looked inside, she asked, "Do you always get up this early?"

"No."

"Do you have to go to work today?" Shoshanna straightened, milk carton in hand, and met her mother's gaze. "We really need to talk. I need to tell you what happened to me while I was away."

Leah wasn't sure she wanted to talk. She didn't think she wanted to hear what had happened to her daughter for the past two years. Maybe it was better to live in blissful ignorance. Or was it better to know all, no matter how painful it might be?

"Just for one day, Mom?"

"Yes," she relented. "I can stay home today."

"Thanks." Shoshanna returned to the table. After she sat down again, she poured a generous portion of milk into her mug and stirred it with a spoon before taking a sip. "Mmm. This is really good."

"You didn't used to drink coffee."

"I was too young. You wouldn't let me. Remember?"

Leah lowered her gaze, staring into the mug clenched between her two hands. "Where did you go, Sho? How did you manage to live?"

"I was in Portland most of the time."

"Portland."

"I lived with friends and got a job working at a used bookstore."

Were you scared? Did anyone hurt you? Did you—?

"It was a guy at the bookstore who led me to Christ."

Leah straightened and gazed at her daughter.

Shoshanna smiled. "I became a Christian a few months ago."

"What on earth do you mean? You've been a Christian since you were a little girl."

"No, Mom." Her smile vanished. "I wasn't."

"Don't be absurd. I remember the day you were confirmed as clearly as if it were yesterday."

Shoshanna got up from the table and went to the sliding glass door, staring outside as Leah had done earlier. "I knew all about Jesus from Sunday school and knew all the right things to say and what I was *supposed* to believe. But I never knew *him*. Not personally. I never made him my Lord and Savior. I never had the joy of the Lord." Her daughter turned. She was smiling again, a twinkle in her eyes. "My friend Greg calls me a turbo Christian now." She laughed softly. "You know, like a big souped-up engine, all revved and ready to go. I want to share Jesus with *everybody!*"

"You're not going to start preaching on street corners, I hope."

"Would it be easier for you if I talked about sex and drugs?" There was a note of confusion in Shoshanna's voice.

Leah's mouth tasted as dry as sawdust. She hadn't meant to sound sarcastic, but neither could she take back her uncharitable retort.

"I did a lot of dumb things while I was gone." Her daughter took two steps toward the table. "But by the grace of God, I wasn't hurt. I had friends who weren't as lucky. They'll never get a second chance."

In an instant, Leah's mind replayed her secret fears. Even now, with Shoshanna safely home, they loomed large and terrifying, too real to contemplate.

"I came home because God's Word says I'm to honor my mother and father, and I needed to make things right with you. I don't know how I'm supposed to do that." She sat on the chair, then leaned toward Leah across the table. "Most of all, I wanted to be able to tell you about what's happened, about the joy I've found in meeting and knowing Jesus."

Leah pressed her lips together, biting back another sharp retort. How dare Shoshanna sit there, with that ring in her nose and those horrid tattoos marring her body, and talk about God and Jesus? As if she knew something Leah didn't. Honor her mother? Make things right?

"Mom?"

"If you really want to make things right with me, you'd take that ugly thing out of your nose."

Shoshanna looked as if she might argue. Then she nodded. "Okay. If it'll make you feel better, I won't wear it when I'm with you."

"Well, it's hard to take anything you say seriously when I'm forced to look at it." Leah felt like a petulant child, only serving to add fuel to her swirl of emotions—relief and irritation and confusion all at once. "Too bad you can't get rid of those tattoos as easily."

"I wish you'd try to see the inside of the cup."

"What is that supposed to mean?"

"It's something from the Bible. It's about—"

"The Bible?"

Shoshanna shook her head. "Never mind, Mom." She stood once again. "We've probably said all we should for now." She turned and walked toward the kitchen doorway. She paused and glanced over her shoulder. "I love you, you know." Then she was gone from view.

The furnace blower shut off. Rain pelted the windows and rushed through the gutters. The coffeepot gurgled and sputtered.

I wish you'd try to see the inside of the cup.

What *had* she meant by that?

Leah covered her face with her hands. "I only want what's best," she insisted to the empty room. "That's all. One day she'll thank me."

Inside of the cup . . .

"O God, help me."

Soup Kitchens and Miracles

Leah vowed to herself that she wouldn't mention either the nose ring or the tattoos again. Even if she had to bite off the tip of her own tongue, she wouldn't say another word about them. As far as she was concerned, they didn't exist. They weren't there.

Denial wasn't *always* a bad thing. Was it?

Shoshanna's wardrobe, however, was another matter. Leah didn't know what young folks called their style of dress these days—funky, hippie, whatever—but she called it atrocious.

When her daughter, sans nose ring, mentioned over breakfast that she intended to look for a job starting next week, Leah suggested they go to the mall later that morning.

"I've taken the day off. We can get you a new wardrobe and avoid the Saturday crowds."

"It isn't necessary, Mom. I've got plenty of things to wear."

"But I *want* to do it, dear. There's nothing like a new outfit or two to make a woman feel better about herself. Besides, you'll need to look your best when you're job hunting."

Leah's gaze flicked momentarily to Shoshanna's head, then dropped away. Who would hire a girl with a nearly bald head and a tattoo on her scalp?

"Maybe there's work for me to do at Together We Can. I've learned a thing or two about living on the streets with homeless people. I'd like to help others get through the tough times. The same way you've helped them."

Several emotions warred within Leah—dread at the thought of her co-workers seeing her daughter's tattoos; pride that she wanted to emulate the work that meant so much to her mother; horror at the confirmation that Shoshanna had lived on the streets under God-only-knows conditions.

"Sounds like a good idea," Wes interjected from his side of the table. "You're always saying you could use more help at the office."

"That's true." Leah met Shoshanna's gaze. "But we can't pay much. We're mostly a volunteer organization, and our goal has always been for ninety percent of our fund raising to go directly to the people in need rather than to administrative costs."

Her daughter shrugged. "It isn't the money that's important. I just want to do something useful. I didn't come home so I could bum off you guys."

"It's settled then." Leah's smile felt a bit uncertain. "We'll go shopping for some appropriate office attire for you. Then Monday you can talk to Carlotta in Personnel. She'll have to make the final decision."

"Don't worry, honey," Wes said to Shoshanna as he placed an arm around his stepdaughter's shoulders. "I'll put in a good word for you with the boss." He punctuated his remark with a conspiratorial wink for Leah and a hug for Shoshanna.

Judging by the number of cars in the mall parking lot, Beaker Heights Towne Square was the place to be on a rainy Friday morning. Leah pulled her Mazda into an open spot, then pushed the button to unlock the doors.

"I brought an umbrella for you," she said as she reached into the back seat.

"It's okay." Shoshanna opened her car door. "A little bit of rain won't make me melt, and it sure won't hurt my hair."

Leah didn't want to talk about her daughter's hair—or lack thereof. Being reminded defeated her new policy of complete denial.

Let it pass. Don't say a thing.

She got out of the car, opened her umbrella, and followed Shoshanna toward the mall's main entrance. Once inside, she tried to steer them in the direction of her favorite department store. Upscale but not ostentatious. Her daughter obviously had another destination in mind.

Leah had never been in Retrospect before. To tell the truth, she wasn't sure she'd noticed its existence.

Raucous music blared from speakers in the ceiling, but Shoshanna didn't seem to mind the noise. She headed directly for a rack of long, bright colored skirts and began poking through them. "How do you like this one?" She held up one for Leah to see.

"Well . . ." She knew she sounded skeptical.

"If I put it with a vest—"

"Wouldn't you like to see what's available at Nordstrom's? I'm sure they've got a great selection for young people."

"Nordie's isn't my style, Mom. This is." Shoshanna raised an eyebrow. "It'd be okay at your office, wouldn't it?"

Leah had to admit there wasn't anything wrong with the skirt or the vests on the neighboring rack. It simply wasn't what she'd had in mind.

Before she could reply, a clerk appeared on the other side of the rack from Shoshanna. "Would you like to try that on?"

Shoshanna looked at Leah, and after a moment, Leah nodded.

"Yes," her daughter said, facing the clerk with a smile. "In a little while. But I'll look for a few more things first."

"There are some great blouses over there you might want to try." The clerk pointed.

"Thanks." Shoshanna began rifling through the skirts again.

"Hey, I've gotta tell you. I love your hair. Wish I could wear mine that short." The young woman leaned forward. "Is that a tattoo on your scalp?"

Leah wanted the floor to open up and swallow her.

Shoshanna laughed. "Yeah, it is."

"Cool."

Another customer, a girl about the same age as Shoshanna, moved closer to Leah, attempting to appear disinterested but obviously wanting a better look.

The clerk asked, "Did it hurt?"

"A little. Mostly it sort of reverberated."

That's because there's nothing between your ears. Leah wished the clerk would shut up and go away.

But she didn't go away. Instead, she said, "I've been wanting a tattoo forever. Everybody's getting them these days."

"Not in my house," Leah muttered to herself.

The other young customer turned wide brown eyes in her direction. "I got grounded when I had my ears double-pierced. My parents would *die* if I got a tattoo."

I know just how they'd feel.

Shoshanna turned toward her mother. She must have guessed what Leah was thinking, for her smile disappeared.

Pricked by her conscience, Leah looked down at the rack of clothes in front of her. She held up the first thing her hand fell upon, paying no attention to what it was. "What about this one?"

"I don't think so, Mom." There was a note of hurt in Shoshanna's voice. "I'm gonna try on what I've got here."

Leah looked up in time to see her daughter working her way through the racks toward the dressing rooms.

I didn't mean to hurt her. But am I so wrong to feel the way I do?

Maybe she didn't want to know the answer.

Clean Cups

"*It's a real* miracle, isn't it?" Rebekah Borders, the pastor's wife, said as she shook Leah's hand following Sunday's service. "Thank you, God, for bringing Shoshanna safely home."

"Yes."

"There's such joy in her eyes."

Leah looked across the narthex to where Shoshanna stood with Josh Borders, Eugene and Rebekah's oldest son.

"It can only be the joy of the Lord," the pastor's wife was saying. "One day I hope she'll share her story with us. I'm sure we would all be blessed by it."

"Perhaps some day," Leah replied softly before moving on.

She exchanged a few perfunctory good mornings with other members of the congregation as she made her way toward the front doors of the church, shook a few more hands, agreed with those who said how wonderful it was that her daughter had returned.

But in Leah's heart, there was disquiet, and she couldn't for the life of her say why.

Rebekah Borders was right about the joy on Shoshanna's face. Leah had observed it throughout the service, particularly during the worship time. While singing, Shoshanna had turned her face toward heaven, oblivious to those around her. It was as if she'd been transported to another dimension.

Had Leah ever experienced that same sort of total abandon during a church service? No, she never had. It wouldn't have been dignified. Church was a place for sober reflection, a place to receive instructions on how to live.

A turbo Christian. Those had been Shoshanna's descriptive words. Well, that was fine for the young, Leah supposed, but faith without works was dead. Being a Christian meant sacrifice and service. It meant being an example to others. Shoshanna would learn in time that it did matter what others thought of her.

Leah stepped outside. Bright sunshine beat down upon the front steps of the church, its warmth moderated by a crisp March wind.

The door opened behind her. "Hey, Mom."

She glanced over her shoulder.

"Do you care if I don't go with you and Dad to lunch?"

"Well, I—"

"I've been invited to go with the youth group to help at the soup kitchen this afternoon. I'd really like to. I'll get a ride home from somebody."

Leah was struck in that instant with a difficult truth: Shoshanna was never going to be her little girl again. They couldn't return to a simpler, more innocent time, before body piercing and tattoos and an absence of two years. Shoshanna was a young woman, not a child, and although she had returned home, Leah couldn't hold her there. She couldn't mold her into her own image. She couldn't make a miniature Leah Carpenter out of her, no matter how hard she tried.

"It's all right, isn't it?" Shoshanna asked again. "You don't mind?"

Leah realized her daughter could have wanted to spend the day hanging out at the mall or making out with some boy or smoking pot or a hundred things worse. Instead, she wanted to help at a community soup kitchen, caring for those less fortunate than herself.

Perhaps Leah hadn't completely failed as a mother.

The next morning, Shoshanna appeared at the breakfast table wearing one of the new outfits from Retrospect. The ankle-length floral skirt was topped by a hot-pink blouse with peasant sleeves and a drawstring neckline, and the purple vest had tassels in front and back. Except for her short-short hair, she looked like a folk singer from the sixties or seventies.

Leah started humming "Monday, Monday" as she served breakfast.

Wes grinned as he met her gaze across the table. "Exactly the one I was thinking of."

The two of them broke into song, making up new lyrics when they couldn't remember the exact words. Finally, unable to continue, they collapsed into laughter.

"You guys are weird," Shoshanna pronounced when the room was silent again.

"*We're* weird?" Leah arched her eyebrows, pretending to be insulted. Seeing Wes's expression, she burst into laughter a second time.

Half an hour later, as they left the house, Wes pulled Leah into an embrace and kissed her with delicious tenderness. Then, with his mouth near her ear, he said, "It's good to see you smiling."

Have I done it so little? she wondered as she met his gaze again.

Yes, she answered herself. She had.

Wes gave her another quick kiss, saying, "You'd better go. You'll get caught in the worst of morning traffic if you don't." He looked beyond Leah toward the Mazda. "Good luck with the interview, honey," he called to Shoshanna. "Be nice to the boss, and I think you've got a good chance at landing a job. She's a bit weird, sings really old tunes, but I think you can handle her okay."

Leah playfully punched him on the arm.

He grunted, then grinned. "Have a great day, honey."

"I intend to."

"Want that Chinese take-out tonight?"

"Sounds great."

The heels of her spectator pumps clicked against the sidewalk as she strode to her car. Opening the rear driver's side door, she placed her leather briefcase on the floor. Moments later, seated behind the steering wheel, she started the engine and backed out of the drive.

Once they were out of the subdivision and into the flow of traffic headed into the city, Leah cast a furtive glance in her daughter's direction. She wondered if Shoshanna was nervous about this morning's interview with the personnel manager. If she was, she didn't show it.

I would have been terrified at her age. She returned her gaze to the road ahead, marveling at another change in her daughter.

"I can't get over how much Beaker Heights has grown in a couple years," Shoshanna said, breaking the silence. "Those are all new subdivisions over there."

"Yes, we've enjoyed all the growth in spite of a flat economy." Leah flipped on her turn signal and changed lanes. "But all the problems that go with it. So many homeless and hungry. So many women living in poverty. So many fatherless children."

"What an opportunity to share our hope in Christ."

Leah glanced at her daughter again.

"'It is for this we labor and strive,'" Shoshanna quoted, looking out the window to her right, "'because we have fixed our hope on the living God, who is the Savior of all men, especially of believers.'"

Leah felt a twinge of guilt. Had she ever offered her faith to someone as a reason for hope? Or had she depended only upon good food, better clothing, and an education to make the difference for the women and children who came to Together We Can?

What kind of Christian am I?

It was not a question that brought comfort, so she shoved it aside. Besides, God helped those who helped themselves. Right? Leah gave others the tools with which to improve their circumstances, and that was important. Give a man a fish, and he has food for a day. Teach a man to fish, and he can feed himself forever. Everyone recognized that truism.

"Does Ms. Rodriguez know I'm coming in this morning?" Shoshanna asked.

"Yes. And remember, she won't hire you unless she thinks you can do the job. That's why she's in charge of personnel."

"Well, if I don't get hired to work in the office, I can still volunteer to help at the shelter."

"Of course."

"It's working with people I want to do anyway. I mean, I know paperwork's important and all, but it isn't what makes the real difference." She sighed. "You know, Mom, if nobody'd reached down into the mire I was living in and showed me a better way, if Greg hadn't shared the good news about how much Jesus loves me, I'd probably be dead by now."

Leah felt her body stiffen, and she clutched the steering wheel like it was her only lifeline.

Shoshanna's voice softened to a near whisper. "Someday, Mom, I hope you'll let me tell you about what happened while I was away. I know you're not ready to hear all of it yet. But someday I hope you will be."

A Dilemma

Leah opened the large glass door to the mauve-and-teal lobby of Together We Can. The receptionist looked up and smiled.

"Morning, Mrs. Carpenter."

"Good morning, Barbara."

Behind her, Shoshanna released a soft whistle. "I thought you said most of the money raised didn't go to overhead. This is nothing like your old offices."

Leah smiled as she glanced over her shoulder. "It doesn't cost us a dime. The attorneys who own the building give it to us rent-free. They get good public relations and a nice tax write-off, and we have the space we need to accomplish our work." She motioned with her hand. "We did all the decorating ourselves, of course."

Even if she tried, she couldn't keep the note of pride out of her voice. The space might be donated, but she had spent a great deal of time and energy designing and decorating these offices. She'd chosen soft colors, wanting to make the place seem comforting, inviting. She'd also wanted to make a statement of success, something she'd discovered attracted more donations.

Glancing back at the receptionist, she said, "Barbara, this is my daughter, Shoshanna. She has an appointment with Ms. Rodriguez at 8:30. When she's ready, please have Carlotta buzz my office."

"I'll tell her, Mrs. Carpenter."

"Follow me, Sho." Leah moved through the lobby, headed for her office at the end of a long hallway. "That room is used for training classes. We instruct women who've never been in the job market how to conduct themselves during an interview." She motioned with her hand. "At the other end of the building we've got a computer lab where we teach basic computing and office skills. And this room is where we help women find the right clothes to wear." She stopped and opened the door, revealing a large room with racks and racks of clothing. "We give every woman who finishes our course a new suit or an appropriate dress to wear on their job hunts. The clothes aren't new, but they look it. You'd be amazed at what some people give away."

"Aren't the women you help a bit intimidated by this fancy office?"

"Some are at first, but most get over it." She continued down the hall. "Our largest women's shelter is two blocks away. We offer childcare so the mothers can come here to attend their classes."

"How long after they get jobs can they stay in the shelters?"

Leah opened the door to her office. "Up to a year."

"Good. There was a place in Portland that only let them stay for a month after employed. That's not near long enough."

"No, you're right—it isn't."

Sho's only eighteen. She shouldn't know so much about the destitute and downtrodden. She should be finishing her high school education and preparing for college in the fall. I wanted so many things for her. I had so many dreams. . . .

Arriving at her desk, Leah stepped behind it, then turned.

Shoshanna had stopped at the bookcase near a large plate-glass window. Morning sunlight gilded her short-cropped hair and revealed a thoughtful crease in her forehead as she perused the titles on the eye-level shelf.

"This is quite a collection, Mom." She tapped her chin with her index finger. "Maybe I can borrow some to look over."

A bit too advanced for a high school dropout, but she didn't say it.

"Did I tell you I hope to be a social worker someday?"

Leah tasted defeat. Didn't Shoshanna realize all that she'd thrown away when she ran away from home? Didn't she realize that business rarely hired people with nose rings and tattoos? As for social work, it required a college degree. Didn't she realize that—

"I got my GED while I was in Portland," Shoshanna said, as if reading Leah's thoughts. "Greg helped me. In fact, we were filling out forms to apply to the university when I decided I needed to come home first."

"Who exactly is this Greg? What was he to you?"

"I told you, Mom. I worked with him at the bookstore. He was—is—my friend."

"Did you live with him?" The implied question was understood.

Shoshanna didn't answer at once. She simply stared back at her mother, disappointment in her eyes. At last she said, "No."

Leah's phone buzzed. She jabbed the intercom button. "Yes?"

"Leah, it's Carlotta. Is Shoshanna ready to meet with me?"

"She's ready." Leah punched the button again. To her daughter she said, "Down the hall to your right. Fourth office. Her name is on the door."

Shoshanna opened her mouth to say something. Then, apparently thinking better of it, she nodded, turned, and left the room.

"Best of luck," Leah said, seconds too late, the door already closed behind her daughter.

A half an hour later, Leah stood at the window staring at the street below, when the door opened again.

"Mind if I come in?" Carlotta asked.

"No." She turned around. "How did it go?"

Carlotta, an attractive Hispanic woman in her mid-thirties, steered her motorized wheelchair into the room. "I was impressed," she answered once she stopped opposite Leah's desk. "She's bright and articulate. I think she'll be an asset."

"You offered her a position?"

"I did."

Leah looked toward the door. "Is she waiting outside?"

"No. She said to tell you she'd be back before lunch. She wanted to go over to the shelter and meet some of the women."

"I see."

"Want to tell me what's bothering you?"

Leah released a deep sigh. "I blew it with Sho." She sank onto her desk chair. "I say the wrong things to her. I hurt her feelings. I don't mean to, but I keep doing it again and again." She shook her head. "I'm angry and I'm scared, and I wonder what she did while she was gone and if she's going to be okay, and I fear for her future, and—"

"Don't you think you should say all this to her?"

"I'm afraid to."

"Why?"

"You know why. We see the reasons every day. We know what happens to girls who live on the streets." Leah blinked, fighting to keep her tears back. In a whisper she continued, "I don't think I could bear knowing if any of it happened to her."

"But every time you look at that tattoo on her scalp, you wonder."

Leah looked at her colleague a long moment, then nodded.

Carlotta's gaze was full of wisdom and sympathy. "You know, my friend. It could be that God can make better use of Shoshanna with the way she looks and who she is than he ever has been able to with you or me. We're so conventional, so conservative." She chuckled. "Shoshanna isn't."

"No, she certainly isn't."

"Maybe it's all part of some grand design. God is turning the mistakes of her past into good."

"Sounds like something Sho would say."

"I get the feeling she's wise beyond her years, Leah. And her faith in God is great. She shared a little bit with me about that. How thankful you must be, to know she's embraced the Lord."

Leah rose a second time, returning to the window. She remembered the way Shoshanna had seemed during worship the previous morning. She thought about the expression of joy and wonder on her face. She wondered again if she'd ever known the same joy, the same peace, that her daughter had found. Carlotta seemed to understand Sho's experience. Why didn't she?

For as long as she could remember, Leah had sought to please God with the way she lived, with the work she did. She believed in Christ, had asked him to live in her heart when she was a little girl. She'd always gone to church, had made it an important part of her life. She prayed. Not as often as she should, she supposed, but she did pray. She read the Bible whenever she found time. It was hard when she had a husband and a home and a business to run and people who were dependent upon her. God had to understand how busy she was. And it didn't make her any less of a Christian.

Did it?

But Shoshanna seemed to have found something . . . more.

I'm envious of her.

The realization stunned Leah—and left her very unsettled.

Politics and Hearts

On Friday afternoon, at the end of Shoshanna's first week at Together We Can, Leah looked for her daughter in the file room, thinking the two of them might leave for home early. Shoshanna was nowhere to be found.

"She finished the work I had for her," Cindy Markowitz said in answer to Leah's query, "so she went over to the shelter." The secretary smiled. "That's where her heart is, you know."

Leah nodded. "Yes, I know. She's told me so more than once. But she needs some practical office experience. She already has several strikes against her if she ever wants to work for someone else. Between her . . . unusual . . . appearance and no high school diploma, she'll have a tough time finding employment from someone other than her mother."

Cindy hesitated a moment, looking uncertain. Finally she asked, "Would you like me to call the shelter? Have them send her back?"

"No, thanks. I'll walk over. It's a nice day out, and it wouldn't hurt to stretch my legs a bit." Leah turned. "Have a nice weekend, Cindy."

"You do the same."

Downtown Beaker Heights was a pleasant blend of the old and the new. Restored sandstone buildings—including some on the Historical Registry—resided beside new high rises of glass, steel and brick. Even here, in the core of the city, trees lifted leafy branches toward the blue, cloudless sky. Daffodils and tulips in large clay pots brightened the sidewalks.

Stepping out of the back door, Leah drew in a deep breath of spring air. Then she turned in the direction of the TWC women's shelter. A soft breeze tugged at her hair and the hem of her skirt as she followed the sidewalk, glancing at the displays in the shop windows.

It had been a good week, she mused. She hadn't expected it to go so well. She'd anticipated problems that hadn't happened, most of them to do with Shoshanna's appearance. Every time she'd introduced her daughter to someone new, she'd gritted her teeth, expecting to see a look of disdain or censure. But if anyone was surprised by Shoshanna's shorn hair or the visible tattoo on her scalp, they hadn't let on.

Of course, those people were Leah's friends and business associates. They would do their best to hide their true feelings. The rest of the world wouldn't be as kind. She was convinced of that. If Shoshanna really wanted to get into social work, to have a professional career, she would have to conform to accepted business standards.

How did she help her daughter see that truth?

Worrying her lower lip between her teeth, she turned the corner onto Elm Avenue. One block away, she saw Shoshanna—her near-naked head made her easy to identify at a distance—sitting on the front stoop of one of the turn-of-the-century brownstones that housed the TWC Family Center. She wasn't alone. Someone was seated beside her. The two were deeply engrossed in conversation. As Leah drew closer, she saw the other person was female and pregnant. She was dressed all in black, from her skin-tight leggings to the sweater stretched over her enlarged stomach.

Leah's footsteps on the sidewalk alerted them to her arrival. Shoshanna turned to look over her shoulder. The other girl—who looked younger than Shoshanna—leaned forward.

Leah slowed, then stopped.

The pregnant girl had metallic purple hair, heavily gelled and spiked. There were two silver rings in her nose and one in her left eyebrow, and she wore black eye shadow and black lipstick. A dog collar circled her throat. *Absolutely ghoulish.*

"Mom . . ." Shoshanna had glanced in her direction and stood. "Do you remember Annie Layton?"

"Layton?"

"We used to live next door to them when I was at Lincoln Elementary. Remember?"

Councilman Layton's daughter?

Howard Layton was one of Together We Can's biggest supporters. More than once he had praised TWC in the press. He often referenced the importance of programs that helped strengthen the family unit.

And this is his daughter?

Annie rose awkwardly from the step. She placed both hands on her abdomen. "Hi, Mrs. Carpenter. Sho told me you got married again. Congratulations."

"Thank you, Annie." Leah managed a response while still trying to reconcile this counterculture teen with the sweet child she'd once known—and the man who was her father.

"Did you need me back at the office?" Shoshanna was asking. "I was hoping to show Annie around the shelter, if you don't mind." With her eyes, she seemed to add, *Please, Mom.*

Leah nodded. "Sure—go ahead. I'll meet you here when you're through."

"Thanks." Shoshanna slipped her hand into the crook of Annie's arm. "Come on. I'll give you the grand tour."

After they'd disappeared inside, Leah sat on a bench in the shade of an elm tree.

Why had Annie Layton come to see Shoshanna? As far as Leah knew, the two girls hadn't seen each other since elementary school. Had they met by chance? Would Shoshanna renew an old friendship with this obviously troubled girl?

With a shudder, Leah closed her eyes. Was Annie the sort of person her daughter had been friends with in Portland? If so, it was nothing short of a miracle that she'd survived her two years in that city.

O God, how do I keep Sho safe now?

The answer she heard deep inside wasn't the one she wanted.

Half an hour later, Shoshanna came out the front door of the shelter. She was alone.

Leah rose from the bench and waited for her daughter to join her on the sidewalk. "Where's Annie?"

"She's staying."

Leah's mouth went dry. She hadn't considered the possibility that Annie Layton had come to the shelter looking for a place to stay. She should have realized it. Of course—young, rebellious, pregnant.

And the daughter of one of the city's most prominent politicians.

"Tell me what happened," Leah said, trying to focus her thoughts.

"She lost her job and couldn't pay the rent. Nobody'll hire her because she's pregnant."

Not to mention the way she looks. "How old is she?"

"Seventeen next week." Shoshanna turned and started walking.

Leah fell in beside her. "Is she using illegal drugs?"

"I don't think so." She glanced at her mother. "Not everybody who looks like her does, you know."

Leah ignored the comment. "Is she married to the baby's father?"

"No, and they aren't together anymore either. She said he left town, and she doesn't know where he went. He took off one day and she hasn't seen him since."

"I'll have to notify her father that she's at the shelter."

"She doesn't want him to know where she is. Beside, I don't think he'll care."

A heaviness pressed on Leah's heart. Her lips felt stiff as she asked, "Is that what you thought about me when you were gone? That I didn't care?" The questions came out of nowhere, surprising her. She didn't have the courage to look at Shoshanna to see if she was equally surprised. Softly, she continued, "Because I did care, Sho. I cared desperately."

There was a lengthy silence, then, "This is different, Mom. Annie's dad really doesn't care."

"How can you be sure?"

"Because he told her he didn't."

"Howard Layton? I don't believe it. He's a very well-respected member of this community. Everyone thinks highly of him. He donates to our organization—"

"People aren't always what they seem."

Leah sent a sidelong glance at her daughter. "It's possible Annie misunderstood what he said, isn't it?"

"I don't think so."

As if it were yesterday, Leah recalled the night before Shoshanna ran away. They'd exchanged heated words, but Leah hadn't suspected the argument would cause her daughter to leave home.

Annie's father must be worried sick about his wayward child. It was doubtful he would come looking for her at the TWC Family Center. It wasn't the sort of place where kids like Annie usually took refuge.

Another thought sprang to mind. She shook her head. "Wouldn't the press have a heyday with this?"

Shoshanna came to an abrupt halt. "Is that what you're worried about? The *press?*" She made it sound like a swear word.

"I have to be concerned about what—"

"Mom, Annie's in trouble. She might look tough, but she's just a kid. She needs help. That's what's important here. Not what the papers might say."

Leah placed a hand on Shoshanna's shoulder. "I'm very aware of that. I also know Annie's a minor and that her father is a powerful member of our city government. The press could use this against him if they chose. If they do, that could hurt the work we do. We're dependent upon fund raising and the benevolence of donors. We have to stay above reproach. If we get bad press, the donations could dry up overnight."

Her daughter made a noise of frustration.

"Like it or not, I must let Councilman Layton know where Annie is. I'll have to call him tomorrow." She paused a moment, then added, "This is in Annie's best interests, too."

Whose Gift?

Late on Saturday morning, Leah was shown into Howard and Donita Layton's formal living room by a uniformed housemaid.

"Make yourself comfortable, Ms. Carpenter," the young woman said. "I'll tell Mr. Layton you're here." She slipped from the room, all sounds of departure muted by thick carpeting.

The Layton home—an impressive, two-story, glass-and-brick structure—sat on a bluff overlooking the swift-flowing Juniper River. Ceiling-to-floor windows formed the south side of the living room, affording an awe-inspiring view of Beaker Heights and the valley beyond.

Leah hesitated beside an off-white, overstuffed chair, then crossed to the window instead of sitting down. She stared down at the sun-sparkled river below, thinking how pleasant it must be to sit on the deck beside the swimming pool on a summer's evening and look over the valley.

"Leah Carpenter," Howard said from behind her. "Great to see you. It's been too long."

Leah turned toward the councilman, a large bear of a man at least six-four and well over two hundred pounds. Fiftyish, he had thick, salt-and-pepper hair that was stylishly cut and a smile that had won him thousands of votes over the years.

"Good morning, Councilman." Leah shook his hand. "Thank you for seeing me on such short notice."

He motioned toward a chair. "Please, have a seat. I've asked Nancy to bring us some coffee."

"That wasn't necessary. I—"

He waved off her words. "I assume my secretary told you Donita is out of town."

Leah didn't reply, realizing it was a rhetorical question.

"My wife goes to New York every spring to shop." He flashed his charming smile. "It's especially important in an election year, you know."

"I'm sure it is." She returned his smile but felt oddly uncomfortable.

"Ah, here's our coffee." He pointed to the cherry wood table in front of him. "Just put the tray there, Nancy. We'll pour it ourselves."

As soon as the maid had excused herself, Howard leaned forward over the table and asked, "Cream or sugar?" He filled a delicate china cup with coffee from the sterling silver pot.

"No, thank you. Black is fine."

He grinned as he passed the cup and saucer to her. "We make it strong in this household, but you strike me as the sort of woman who'd like it that way. Am I right?"

Her discomfort increased. She'd never noticed how smooth, slick, he seemed.

"Now tell me." Howard leaned back in his chair. "What brings you to my home? I assume this has something to do with Together We Can. How can I help?"

Leah put the cup back in the saucer, her coffee untouched. "You're partially right, Councilman. It does have something to do with Together We Can."

He gave her one of those enigmatic looks peculiar to politicians, one expressing curiosity and tolerant patience at the same time.

"Your daughter is at one of our shelters."

"My daughter?" His expression froze in place.

"Annie."

"What's she doing there?" His voice was like granite, cold and hard.

"She said she had nowhere else to go."

He made a gruff sound. "I'm not surprised." He rose from the chair and strode toward the windows. Squinting against the bright sunlight, he said, "I told her this would happen when she went to live with that no-good boyfriend of hers. I told her he'd get tired of her and throw her out."

Leah clenched her hands in her lap. "Are you aware she's expecting a baby?"

"Of course I'm aware of it. The little twit didn't have enough sense to prevent it."

"We . . . our shelters aren't designed to meet the needs of expectant teens."

"Then kick her out. You've got your rules. Stick to 'em. Tell her to go."

Leah drew back as if he'd struck her. "But, Councilman Layton, you can't mean—"

"No. You're right, Ms. Carpenter." He turned to face her. "You can't throw her out."

Leah released the breath she'd been holding.

"Wouldn't look good. We'll need to get her out of town quietly instead." He muttered a curse. "I offered to pay for an abortion when she first told me she was in trouble. She refused. Can you believe it? Refused."

"There are other options besides abortion."

"Not if she wants to come home again. She knew what was expected of her, and she defied me." He swore again. "She made her bed, she can very well lie in it. Don't expect me to clean up this mess. It'll be all I can do to keep it out of the evening news." He drew a deep breath. "Why she couldn't just get lost like thousands of other teens do every year? And this an election year, to boot."

Leah stared at the man, unable and unwilling to believe what she was hearing.

What was it Shoshanna said yesterday? People weren't always what they seemed. That was certainly true of Howard Layton. Leah had heard him speak against abortion more than once. In fact, he'd voiced many of her own political and moral beliefs in his speeches and public appearances. She'd admired him and had been thankful for his support for Together We Can.

But now . . .

She rose from her chair, clutching her purse with both hands. "Thank you for your time, Councilman. We'll do whatever we can to help Annie. Don't worry. The press won't hear anything from us."

Leah was halfway home before she decided to turn the car around and go to the Family Center instead.

She hadn't a clue what she intended to do about Annie. TWC provided shelter and training for women in need. Many had been battered. Almost all lacked education and training. TWC's goal was to help them enter the work force, to get them off food stamps and welfare and enable them to provide for themselves and their children, if they had any—and most did.

At this stage of her pregnancy, Annie really couldn't be trained until after the baby was born. And what then? Did she mean to keep the baby? Surely not. Not only was she awfully young, but she would be an unsuitable mother. One only had to see her purple hair and hideous makeup to know that was true. No, she had to be encouraged to place her baby for adoption.

Leah shook her head, reminding herself that once Howard Layton removed Annie from the Family Center, she would no longer be Leah's concern.

But what if he didn't take her from the shelter?

I'll call Beaker Memorial as soon as I get to the center. Maybe we can move her today. She'll get good prenatal care there, and they'll counsel her about adoption. There's no reason the councilman has to send her out of town. Beaker Memorial is discreet.

It was the logical course of action. An appropriate plan. So why didn't she feel satisfied with it? She was still pondering that question when she arrived at the shelter.

Inside the entrance of the Family Center, Leah greeted the receptionist at the front desk, then asked what room Annie had been assigned.

"Twenty-seven, Ms. Carpenter. Your daughter's up there now."

"Shoshanna's here?"

"Yes, ma'am. Arrived about fifteen minutes ago. Maybe half an hour."

"Thanks." She turned and headed for the staircase.

She shouldn't be spending so much time with Annie. What if it makes her miss whatever sort of life she lived in Portland? But if I forbid her to see Annie, it could backfire. It might be worse. She might decide to—

She stopped herself before she could think the unthinkable.

Oh, God, how do I find the answers? How do I know what's the right thing to do?

As if in answer to her silent prayer, she heard Shoshanna's voice through the open doorway of room twenty-seven. "At the foot of the cross. That's the only place to go for real help, Annie. To the foot of the cross."

At the foot of the cross. The words echoed in Leah's heart. That's the only place to go for real help. To the foot of the cross.

Leah stopped before reaching the doorway, holding still and listening.

"I can't tell you that turning your life over to Christ will make any difference with your dad," Shoshanna continued, her voice low but clear. "I *can* promise it'll make all the difference in you."

Annie voice. "I tried going back to church once. It wasn't for me. You know how your mom looked at me yesterday? That's the way they looked at me in that church I went to. I don't fit in."

Shoshanna laughed softly. "Jesus spent all his time with people who didn't fit in. The outcasts. The poor. The tax collectors. The lepers. The prostitutes. The people society didn't care for. The ones who couldn't measure up. He loved them the way they were, but he didn't leave them that way."

"I've had enough of hypocrites." Annie's voice rose, tinged with bitterness. "Dad only goes to church 'cause it's good for votes. He doesn't believe in any religion far as I can tell. Bet there are plenty like him in those places."

"You're right, Annie. The church has its share of hypocrites, but nobody ever said Christians were perfect. People are people. They'll disappoint you all the time. Even the ones who love you most are going to fail you, the same way you'll fail them, even when you don't mean to. But Christ won't ever fail you. Not ever."

Leah heard the calm assurance in Shoshanna's words and pictured the patient smile on her face.

"Jesus doesn't expect you to be perfect the way some people do. He won't judge you if you look different, the way your dad does. He won't ever send you away if you make a mistake. God isn't sitting up there in heaven, waiting to smack you down when you mess up. He wants to help you become everything he wants you to be. He wants to love you and to have you love him. That's where true Christianity starts. With love."

Her daughter's words cut straight to Leah's heart. She felt suddenly lost and alone.

"You can't earn your way to heaven," Shoshanna's voice continued, "no matter how many good things you do. Not even if you twist yourself inside out. Not even if you manage to please your dad a hundred percent of the time."

With tears in her eyes, Leah turned and walked away from the half-open door.

A full moon bathed the neighborhood in a white glow, casting long, inky shadows behind objects large and small. March-bare tree limbs waved their arms in a ghostly dance while the wind whistled around eaves and down chimneys.

Leah observed the night scene through the bedroom window, her arms hugged her midsection.

I wish you'd try to see the inside of the cup.

She'd found the passage in the Gospel of Matthew. Now she wished she hadn't. The words seemed to scream at her, accusing her.

Woe to you, scribes and Pharisees, hypocrites! For you clean the outside of the cup and of the dish, but inside they are full of robbery and self-indulgence. You blind Pharisee, first clean the inside of the cup and of the dish, so that the outside of it may become clean also.

"Care to tell me what's troubling you?" Wes asked from the opposite side of the room.

Leah shook her head.

"It's after midnight." He got out of bed and came to stand behind her. "Honey?" He placed a hand on her shoulder.

"Am I a hypocrite?"

"What?"

"Am I a hypocrite?"

He moved his hand from her shoulder to her hair, stroking it gently. "No. Why do you ask?"

"I think maybe I am."

Wes turned her to face him. "Come on. Tell me what's eating at you. You've been moody ever since you got home. Is this about Councilman Layton?"

"No." She shook her head again. "Not really."

"Shoshanna?"

A lump in her throat kept her from answering.

Wes drew her close, pressing the side of her face to his chest, his other hand against the center of her back. "I'm here. Just know that. If you need me, I'm here for you."

She wished she could talk to him, tell him everything. She wanted to. She knew she could trust him. But she couldn't put her thoughts or feelings into words. Not yet. They were all a jumble, part of her overall confusion. She felt raw and exposed, and verbalizing what little she understood would only make that worse.

Reunion Complexities

Leah felt better than she had in more than a week. Nothing like redecorating to restore a woman's spirits. Especially when it was a surprise for her daughter.

Standing in the center of Shoshanna's bedroom, Leah looked around with pleasure. The new furniture—bookcase headboard, bedside table, large desk, and five-drawer dresser—was made of light oak in a contemporary design. It went well with the matching royal blue and yellow flowered comforter, bed skirt, and curtains. A lamp with a yellow shade sat on the bedside table; its twin had been placed on the corner of the desk.

"I should find a print for the wall above the bed," Leah murmured to herself.

She knew the perfect store to find what she wanted. That art gallery at the corner of Swan Falls and Eighth Street. Maybe tomorrow on her lunch hour she could—

"Mom, what's happening here?"

"Sho!" She spun toward the door. "You aren't supposed to be home this afternoon."

"Neither are you." Her daughter stepped into the room. "What have you done with my things?"

"I wanted it to be a surprise. Do you like it?"

Shoshanna met her gaze for a moment, then glanced around the room. "It's pretty," she finally answered, her voice soft, almost inaudible. "Very tasteful."

The response was lackluster at best, and it stung Leah, stealing her pleasure like a bucket of ice water.

"Why'd you do it, Mom?"

Her disappointment turned to anger. "Well, for crying out loud. Don't bother to be grateful or anything. I was just trying to make things nice for you."

"I know that's what you think. But look at it. This is *you,* not me. Don't you see? This is your taste, not mine." Shoshanna pinioned her with a straight gaze. "Is it because you can't change me, so you had to change my room instead?"

"Of course not! Of all the stupid, psychobabble kind of things to say."

Shoshanna's eyes widened.

"I don't know why I bother to do anything nice for you, Sho. Put your old things back if you want. I don't care." She stormed out of the room toward the staircase.

Her daughter followed. "We need to talk about this."

"I don't want to talk about it."

"You've got to let me be who I am, Mom."

She spun around at the top of the stairs. "I'm not trying to keep you from being who you are. All I want to do is to—"

"Change me."

"Why are you fighting with me? Why can't you say thank you and let it go at that?"

"Because you're not going to stop until I'm a carbon copy of you, and I can't be you."

"Am I that bad?"

Shoshanna slowly moved toward her and reached out with one hand. "You're not bad at all. You're just not me." She moved closer. "I didn't mean to hurt your feelings. Really I didn't. It was nice what you tried to do. I just think—"

"I already know what you think," Leah interrupted. "You think you're so smart and know so much more than your mother. Well, I've got news for you, kiddo. You don't know much about anything. You may not want to conform to what our society thinks is acceptable and what isn't, but you'll have to if you want to succeed, if you're going to make anything of yourself in this world." Her voice rose by degrees. "Life is going to knock you down, Sho. It'll knock you down again and again. You're only eighteen. You haven't been there, but I have. I've been around the block a few more times than you, and I know how hard it can be. Can't you see I want to protect you, to make your way a little easier?"

Shoshanna's shoulders slumped. "Maybe easier isn't the way it's supposed to be. Maybe I've got a different kind of path to follow."

There was that horrible out-of-body moment when Leah saw herself, saw her behavior, and was ashamed. Her shame increased when she noticed the tears slip from her daughter's eyes, leaving twin tracks down her cheeks.

I wish you'd try to see the inside of the cup.

Leah winced as she recalled those words. Then a different voice intruded on her thoughts. Her mother's voice.

You'll never amount to anything, Leah Nadine. Despite everything I've done for you, you'll never be what I want you to be.

Leah had tried to be the perfect daughter. From as early as she could remember, she'd done everything she could to please her mother. Yet they'd never been close. The harder Leah tried, the more of a disappointment she'd seemed to be. Her mother was gone now, but the ache, the sense of failure, still remained.

Had she passed on that legacy to Shoshanna? Had the sins of the mother been visited upon the child, like an Old Testament curse? She clutched at the stair railing.

"Oh, God," she whispered beneath her breath, the only prayer she could manage.

Shoshanna was brushing away the tears with her fingertips.

"Forgive me, Sho."

"It's okay."

"No." She shook her head. "It isn't okay. But I want it to be."

The church was cool and dim. The only light was filtered through the stained-glass windows at the front and rear of the sanctuary.

Leah slipped into a back pew. She sat with her hands folded tightly in her lap, staring all the while at the large cross above the altar.

She remembered when they'd hung it there against a backdrop of purple fabric. That was the year after Eugene Borders had come to pastor their church. Leah hadn't cared for him much at the time. He'd made too many changes right from the start. Not that they'd been bad changes, but Leah liked things to be familiar, to hold to tradition. She liked to maintain the status quo whenever possible. She liked to know what every day would bring with it so she could plan and prepare. Be ready.

She had always tried to control her own life. What a joke that had turned out to be.

Closing her eyes, she let the silence of the sanctuary envelope her. Slowly, the turmoil in her mind and in her heart began to still. After a long while, she opened her eyes again.

The afternoon sun had moved in those minutes of silent reflection, and now the light streamed through the stained glass of the balcony window from a new angle, casting tiny rainbows against the royal-colored cloth, causing a halo effect around the cross.

"Have you the answers for me?" she whispered.

She didn't hear the voice of God reply.

"Have I *ever* heard you? I don't remember. Was there a time when I knew you the way others seem to?" She paused, then added, "The way Sho seems to?"

She closed her eyes again and lowered her chin toward her chest.

I forced her away once before, God. I don't want to do it again. I don't want to make her feel like I'm judging her. . . . But maybe I am judging her. Maybe I am trying to make her into another me. I only want what's best for her.

In her mind, she heard Shoshanna's soft laughter, heard her saying to Annie, "Jesus spent all his time with people who didn't fit in."

That's true, and it's all well and good. But things are different now than they were when Jesus walked the earth. We don't live in the same kind of world. We must care what others think about us if we're to make a difference. If I hadn't cared what others thought, how much would I have been able to accomplish in this community? People give their money to Together We Can because they know they can trust me and my organization. They know it because they can see who I am. So we do need to care. Right?

She looked at the cross again.

"Well, aren't I right?" she challenged aloud.

Leah had a sudden mental image of the councilman, another person who coveted the approval of others, who knew the importance of the public image.

The thought left an unpleasant taste in her mouth.

I'm not like Howard Layton. Look at Together We Can. Look at how it helps people. I'm not doing this for personal glory or to get votes or to make a lot of money. I'm doing it because it's a good thing to help others who are less fortunate. That's the Christian thing to do. That's the essence of the Christian creed.

Outcasts. People who didn't fit in. She'd dedicated her life to helping them.

But do you help them because you love them?

She looked around quickly—had someone else heard the question? *Love them? Well . . .*

Do you help them because you love me, Leah?

She held her breath.

Beloved, do you help them because you know I love you?

Leah sat in her car outside a convenience store two blocks from the church and called home on her cell phone. Shoshanna didn't answer, and Leah got the answering machine instead.

She pressed End, then dialed the office. As soon as she heard the receptionist's greeting, she said, "Barbara, it's Leah Carpenter. I need to talk to my daughter."

"Sorry, Ms. Carpenter," Barbara replied. "Shoshanna won't be back in this afternoon. She said something about helping a friend move."

Leah worried her lower lip.

"I think it was somebody over at the shelter," Barbara continued. "Did she say who?"

"Sorry. No."

"Okay, thanks." Leah flipped the phone closed.

A friend at the shelter meant Annie Layton. Leah was sure of that.

She started the engine and drove out of the parking lot, headed into the downtown area just as the rush to leave the city began. She didn't know what she would say to Shoshanna. She simply knew she couldn't put it off.

But she had one very important stop to make first.

Heart's Homecoming

When Leah turned onto Elm Avenue, she saw Shoshanna carrying a box down the front steps of the shelter. By the time Leah parked her car behind a dented, paint-faded Chevy van, Shoshanna had already set the box inside it. Then she stood beside the vehicle and watched as her mother got out of the car.

Shoshanna's expression was inscrutable.

"Would you like some help?" Leah asked as she stepped onto the curb.

"Thanks, but that's all there is."

"Annie?"

"Yeah."

"Does Beaker Memorial have an opening for her?"

"No, but she didn't want to go there anyway."

Leah looked toward the front stoop of the shelter. "Is she going home then?" How wonderful if the councilman had come to his senses and wanted to do the right thing by his daughter.

"No. I found her a place to stay with a couple I met at church. Maybe you know them. The Stuarts. They've got a little studio apartment in their basement they're going to let Annie use."

A plethora of objections popped into Leah's head. It took great effort not to voice them aloud.

"Can you spare me a few minutes?" she asked as she looked at her daughter once again. "Maybe after you take Annie to the Stuarts?"

Shoshanna shrugged. "Sure. But now's fine if you want. Annie's already over there. I just borrowed the van to get her things for her." She motioned toward the bench beneath the shade tree. "This okay?"

Leah nodded, and the two of them sat down.

Silence stretched between them.

At last, Leah drew a deep breath, met her daughter's gaze, and began. "I've been doing a lot of thinking since I saw you this afternoon. I . . . I think you're right about my reasons for redecorating your room." She sighed as she looked down at her hands, clenched in her lap. "But it went beyond that. I think I was running away from an even greater truth." A lump formed in her throat, making it difficult to continue. "I've been guilty of the sin of pride." Tears flooded her eyes, blurring her vision. "And it's separated me from God for years. Pride made my first love grow cold."

"Oh, Mom, you—"

"No." She held up a hand to stop Shoshanna's protest. "It's true. I've spent most of my Christian life looking at appearances and making judgments and decisions based upon those appearances. I've expected others to do the same. I've expected them to be impressed by the good works that I've done. Why shouldn't they be? Haven't I won awards and been honored by the community? Haven't I been the good Samaritan, saving people from poverty, changing lives? I even expected God to be impressed by all I've achieved." She glanced at her daughter. "It took you coming home for me to take a good hard look at myself and my relationships.

With you. With Wes. With the people at work. And most of all, my relationship with Christ."

Shoshanna took hold of Leah's left hand and gently squeezed it. Forgiveness flowed through the gesture. It flowed straight into Leah's heart, releasing a beautiful peace.

"I . . . I have something for you." Leah reached into her suit coat pocket and removed the small package. She looked at it for a moment, then passed it to her daughter.

Shoshanna opened the mouth of the plain white sack, removed a tiny wad of tissue paper, and slowly unwrapped the gift. When she saw what it was, she looked at Leah once again, her eyes wide with surprise.

Leah laughed nervously. "Never expected something like that from me, did you?"

"No." Shoshanna lifted the small silver hoop from the folds of the tissue paper.

"I don't want you to be me, Sho. I want you to be the wonderful person God made you to be. The unique and special individual he formed in my womb."

Leah reached out, placing both of her hands around her daughter's hand, the one that held the silver nose ring. A simple piece of body jewelry had become a symbol what had taken place in Leah's heart, a symbol only the two of them and God would understand.

"Thanks for helping me see the inside of the cup, Sho. I love you."

Life's Full Circles

Five years later ...

Leah had the door open before the taxi rolled to a stop in front of the hospital. She grabbed her carry-on bag with one hand while shoving two twenty dollar bills at the driver.

"Keep the change," she said, half-sliding, half-stepping from the rear of the cab.

She bypassed the automatic door, knowing it would move too slowly. Once inside, she raced to the information desk.

"May I help you?" a volunteer in a pink and white dress asked.

"My daughter's here. She's having a baby."

"Her name?"

"Shoshanna Borders."

The volunteer glanced down at a computer screen while tapping a few keys. "There's nothing in the system yet. You'll need to check at the desk in delivery. Take the elevator to the second floor, turn right when you come out of the elevator, and go down the hall. You'll be able to see the desk."

"Thanks," she said over her shoulder as she hurried off, gripping her bag and purse and wishing she could be rid of them both.

Lord, please let everything go okay. Please protect Sho and her baby. Let it be a safe and normal delivery.

It was the same type of prayer she'd been lifting to heaven for the past several hours, ever since she received the call from her son-in-law.

"Shoshanna's in labor," Josh had said without a hello.

"Labor? But she isn't due for another three weeks. Are you sure it isn't false labor?"

"We're sure. We're at the hospital now."

"I'll catch the first flight out. I'll be there as soon as I can. Tell Sho I'm coming."

Amazing how long a relatively short flight could seem when a person was in a hurry.

The elevator doors opened. Leah looked up—and there stood Josh, as if he'd been waiting for her. She knew in an instant that all was well. Judging by the large grin on his face, she also guessed she was too late to witness her grandchild's introduction to the world.

"Hi, Mom," Josh greeted her. She stepped out of the elevator and into his embrace.

"Glad you got here okay. Wes coming?"

"No, he couldn't leave today. He'll fly in tomorrow." She drew back so she could look into his eyes. "Well? Don't you have something to tell me?"

"Shoshanna's fine."

"And the baby?"

"You have a beautiful granddaughter."

"A girl." Joy welled in Leah's chest. "A granddaughter."

Josh put his arm around her shoulders. "Come on. I'll take you to them." He guided her down the hall, his long stride shortened to accommodate hers.

Thank you, Father-God, for giving Sho a wonderful man who loves her just the way she is, a man she loves in return. Thank you for putting these two unlikely young people together. I never would have seen it coming, but you knew all along. Just as you know what lies ahead for their new baby.

Josh steered Leah into a room decorated with soft blue wallpaper. Shoshanna lay in the bed, a small bundle held in her arms.

"Mom," she said, sounding both tired and happy. "You made it." Shoshanna's hair was long now because Josh liked it that way. But it was no longer straight and fine. It was a mass of dreadlocks, interspersed with strands of blue extensions.

"I made it." Leah moved toward the bed, her gaze glued to the tiny pink knitted cap on the baby's head. "But I plan to have a long talk with your husband about taking you away from Beaker Heights."

"He already knows. But we have to go—"

"—where the Lord calls," Leah finished for her.

Shoshanna pulled down the receiving blanket with two fingers, revealing the baby's face. "Grandma Leah, meet Chloe Leanne Borders."

* * *

Two hours later, Leah sat in the corner of the hospital room, her granddaughter cradled in her arms. The room was enveloped in silence. Shoshanna slept, and Josh had gone to the church where he was a part-time youth pastor.

Leah smiled as her gaze drifted to her dreadlocked, blonde-and-blue-haired daughter. Shoshanna lay on her side, the tattoo on her right shoulder blade peeking over the top of her nightgown.

"Not exactly the picture of a pastor's wife, huh, Chloe?" She looked down at the newborn. "But what a lovely heart for God beats inside her chest."

Leah's thoughts wandered back through time to the fateful night of the Beaker Heights' Citizen of the Year banquet. She remembered that sick feeling in her stomach when she'd seen her daughter with the tiny silver ring in the side of her nostril. She remembered her anger as she'd argued with Shoshanna later that evening.

"It hurt to look at her." She shook her head, her fingertips stroking the downy softness of the baby's head while she pondered her memories. "Imagine that, Chloe. A silly little ring in her nose was like a pain in my heart that built a wall between us."

Funny how unimportant the tattoos and body jewelry seemed to Leah today. They were mere cosmetics in the overall scheme of things. It was the person underneath who counted. It was the condition of a heart that mattered.

The inside of the cup.

And what a beautiful cup the Lord had made of Shoshanna.

"But I must confess something to you, little one," Leah whispered. "I *am* glad your mommy has hair again, even if some of it is blue."

Smiling, the new grandmother closed her eyes, leaned her head against the back of the chair, and reveled in the never-ending flow of grace that had been poured out for them all.

Her Story Jar

"*So you see,*" Mrs. Halley concluded, her gaze kind upon Beth's face. "God can use any of us. No matter our backgrounds. No matter our flaws. No matter our appearance. All he needs is a willing heart, and he is able to work miracles."

Beth found herself teary-eyed for the second time, more moved by the widow's words than she cared to admit. She reminded herself she was nothing like the mothers in Mrs. Halley's stories. Besides, she was more accustomed to cleaning churches than to sitting in one on a Sunday morning. Not exactly the kind of person God listened to.

"Nothing is impossible with the Lord, my dear," Mrs. Halley said, once again seeming to read Beth's thoughts.

Beth rose from the floor, her muscles complaining over the length of time she'd been sitting there.

Nothing is impossible with the Lord.

She reached for her cleaning bucket. As she did so, that charm bracelet slipped forward with a faint tinkle of metal on metal.

The boys had given the bracelet to her for Christmas five years ago. It wasn't anything fancy, but she prized it above every piece of jewelry she owned. Tommy and Mark had been so proud when she opened that package and exclaimed over their gift. They'd saved their allowance for weeks in order to buy it, then had talked the next-door neighbor into taking them to the mall.

She smiled at the memory, even as tears threatened once more.

Beth wished she had a trinket to add to the story jar, some place in her life that she could be certain had been touched by God's grace. Maybe a charm bracelet would be the perfect thing to put inside, although Beth would never part with this one.

She wished she had enough faith so she wouldn't be shaken in trying circumstances!

Oh, to be able to trust something . . . or Someone . . . you couldn't see.

"Is there anything I can do for you, my dear?" Mrs. Halley asked softly.

It seemed a strange request, coming from a woman who'd recently buried her husband. Yet Beth was certain it was asked with genuine concern. She didn't intend to reply. She knew there was nothing the elderly widow could do to help her. But then, suddenly, the words were there, echoing in the sanctuary.

"Sometimes I feel like such a failure as a mother." Beth stared at the various items in her pail of cleaning products and rags. "Such a complete failure. Maybe I was never meant to be a mother in the first place."

Mrs. Halley leaned toward her from the wing chair and took Beth's hands in her own. Her slender fingers felt cool and sensible, like soft leather. "I can tell how much you love your boys, just from looking at you."

"I do." Beth nodded. She bit her bottom lip and sighed. "I've tried so hard."

Their eyes met and held. For a bit, silence enveloped the pretty little sanctuary. That silence, in itself, spoke volumes. "Perhaps," Mrs. Halley said at last, "the time has come for you to stop trying."

Beth lost the battle with her tears. They ran down her cheeks. "I'm different than the women in those stories." Oh, my, all the cleaning rags she'd brought with her, and not one Kleenex among them. "I guess I just don't have that much faith," she said, her voice breaking.

"Not any of us do, dear. I don't know if I've got the faith to say good-bye and walk out of this room in a few minutes, never to see it again. I don't know if I have the faith to climb out of bed tomorrow morning"—she faltered here, having to say the words—"to face the future without my John."

"I'm so sorry." Beth slipped her hands away. She piled the spray can of polish and a bottle of glass cleaner into her pail. "I've said things that make you sad."

"No, Beth, I'm fine. But faith is never something that we give to ourselves, Beth. Faith is something that the Heavenly Father gives us, just when we need it the most. We have only to ask, and he will answer."

"It's been so long," Beth whispered. "I've forgotten how to ask."

Even though Beth had noted the old woman's steps waver before, she saw her stand now with renewed strength, with the same confidence she'd had when she entered the room. "Would you like me to pray with you?"

Beth nodded. "Please."

"Come, then. It will be my last time to pray for someone here. After so many." Together, the two women walked toward the simple, leaning pulpit. The sunlight against the ivory pews had lengthened to a rich, tranquil expanse of gold. Somewhere, in some place, it was the time when vespers would be sung. Everything in the sanctuary—the lectern, the piano, the rows of hymnals, all perfectly aligned like soldiers—gleamed. In the gentle late-afternoon light, dust motes suspended lightly in the air like swarms of glitter.

"Do you know the Lord as your Savior, Beth?" Mrs. Halley asked.

Beth shook her head. "I don't think so. I've come to church sometimes but, no—"

"Would you like to?"

"Yes."

Together, the two women prayed. For salvation. For faith. For healing. For rest. For acceptance.

At the beginning of the prayer, Beth was afraid. *What if Mrs. Halley expects me to say something? Isn't it important to have the right words when talking to somebody as big as God?*

But halfway through the prayer, without even thinking about it, she found herself praying for Mrs. Halley too. After the final *amen*, as their faces lifted and they smiled with sweet gratitude at one another, Beth thought of something she had never realized before.

Tommy and Mark belong to the Lord. At all turns in their lives, He loves them more than I ever can. They are more his children than they will ever be mine.

The thought staggered her. Overwhelmed her. And released her. She wasn't parenting alone. She never had been. Her boys had a heavenly father to rely on. And so did she.

"Well." Mrs. Halley lifted the jar, encircled it protectively with one arm, and made her way down the carpeted steps from the platform. "I've stayed longer than I planned. There wasn't anybody at home to hurry back for."

When she faltered on the steps, Beth hastened to support the woman, taking her elbow. "Thank you for sharing the story jar with me." Beth gave her a grateful squeeze. "They're such wonderful stories. Perhaps now that you have a little more time, you could write some of them down."

She met Beth's gaze with a smile. "That's a nice thought. Perhaps someday I will."

Mrs. Halley walked down the aisle. Only when she reached the door did she turn back. One last time Beth saw her lift her gaze to the altar, to the pulpit, to all the love and sorrows, the joys and the memories, held before God in such an unadorned, simple place.

"Well," she breathed. That was all. Just one word: *Well.*

And then she was gone.

Beth stood watching after Mrs. Halley, her heart filled with stories from the jar. She realized that what seemed an ending for Mrs. Halley yet marked a beginning for her and her boys.

She'd be back here again. If not to clean, then to worship. It would be a good time to start attending a church. It pleased her, thinking of meeting the new pastor.

Oh, yes. The organ. She'd almost forgotten that she hadn't finished with the dusting. Beth hurried forward and spritzed just a little more polish on the dust rag, and the tang of lemon mingled with the faint perfume of carnations. As she buffed the smudges from the instrument's console, she began to hum to herself.

A song of joy and new beginnings. Maybe she'd start her own story jar.

Tributes to Our Mothers and Grandmothers

From friends and family

A Mother's Gift

by

FRANCINE RIVERS, MOTHER AND AUTHOR

My mother, Frieda King, was a woman devoted to letters and journals. From the time I was a little girl, I can picture her sitting at a small, brown painted desk with three drawers on each side and the top covered with horrendous green vinyl. There she wrote letters to family and friends on stationery along with observations of the day in a spiral notebook. She always used the same beige fountain pen, which she guarded as though made of solid gold set with diamonds.

On family vacations Mom would sit in the front seat of the car with a steno pad and write descriptions of the scenes, finishing the entries during the evening hours. During those early years, it was tent camping and writing by firelight. Later, we camped in small, then larger, travel trailers, and she wrote by blue butane.

My mother was the first to encourage me to write.

She had beautiful penmanship—consistently elegant, with round, slanting letters. As an adult with a home and family of my own, I always knew how Mom was feeling physically and emotionally, not by the words in her letters but by her handwriting. It was a barometer of the storms in her life . . . my brother's capture by the North Vietnamese, my father's heart condition and liver cancer, and finally the dwindling of her strength as she battled breast cancer.

As Mom calmly faced death, she asked what I wanted from the house. I asked for her journals. If I couldn't have her, I wanted her work so I could spend time with her after she had gone to be with the Lord. I considered her worn steno pads and spiral notebooks my most precious inheritance. It wasn't till after her death that I found some short stories and a full-length novel along with letters from a roommate during nurses' training. I then learned that my mother had dreamed of being a professional writer.

Instead of pursuing her dream, she set it aside and became the wind beneath my wings.

The Best Times of Your Life

by

DEBBIE MACOMBER, MOTHER AND AUTHOR

I love babies and big families and always wanted that for my-self. The book and movie I loved was *I Remember Mama.* I decided I wanted a dozen children too. If my husband didn't agree to twelve, then eight—but no fewer.

My feelings about family came from my mother. Connie Adler was the oldest of eight in a second family. (Her mother was a widow with five when she married my grandfather, Florian Zimmerman.) This meant lots of cousins and a large extended family. During the baby-boom years following World War II, there were five of us Adler cousins, all born within a few months of one another. In fact I owe my entire writing career to my brother and two cousins who copied my diary and sold it to boys in my eighth-grade class. It was my first bestseller!

Eighteen months after Wayne and I married, our first daughter arrived. Jody was my parents' first grandchild and the apple of their eye. My mother came for two weeks and helped me adjust to motherhood. The following year when Jenny arrived, my mother came again, as she did when I delivered Ted, then Dale. After four babies in five years, Wayne and I knew we'd reached our emotional and financial limits.

Shortly after our last, Dale, was born, I found myself emotionally and physically worn out. I don't know what I would have done without Mom to help me through this recovery time. All four of the children would sit with me in the rocking chair my father had built, and I'd rock them back and forth, Jody and Jenny on my legs while the two boys shared my lap.

Mother told me about her mother rocking seven children all at one time. Then she looked at me with such joy and said, "Treasure these days, Debbie. These will be the happiest years of your life."

Happiest of my life? I hadn't slept a full night through for several years. I remember looking at my mom and asking, "You mean it gets worse?"

Mom laughed and suggested I wait and see. Now that I'm a grandmother myself, I can appreciate my mother's wisdom. Those were the easy times, when I could cuddle my children close, protect them from the temptations of the world, share with them the wonder of God's love. As I look back on those days, draining as they were, I realize how right she was.

Thanks, Mom, for pointing me toward the future and reminding me to savor what I have right at this moment.

Mom's Old Bible

by

JERRY B. JENKINS,
SON AND AUTHOR

Late one night when I was a teenager, I took a good look at my mother's Bible. The crumbling cover and dog-eared pages brought back memories of my childhood's bedtime prayers when she was "Mommy."

An inscription from Dad dated the Bible from before my birth. Mom's maiden name was barely readable on the cover. Two references were penned on the grimy first page—the first one, John 3:5, unmistakably written by my oldest brother, Jim. The backward scrawl reminded me of those years when the Bible was passed around, carried to church, and claimed as "mine" by four different boys. Mom didn't often get to carry the Bible herself while we were growing up, but we frequently found her reading it at home when we came in from paper routes or baseball games.

The other reference on that first page was Psalm 37:4 in Mom's handwriting. I turned to the Psalm and saw that Mom had underscored the verbs in the first five verses. They admonish:

"Fret not thyself because of evildoers. . . . Trust in the LORD, and do good. . . . Commit thy way unto the Lord; trust also in him; and He shall bring it to pass" (KJV).

Apparently, though, her favorite verse in the passage was *"Delight thyself also in the LORD; and he shall give thee the desires of thine heart"* (KJV).

On the next page the inscription from Dad: "To Bonnie, in loving remembrance of October 21, 1942. Your devoted Red. Matthew 19:6." He'd been nearly nineteen, she sixteen, when they were engaged. World War II and his thirty-two months in the Pacific delayed their marriage until December 1945.

I turned another page. "Hello everybody" in Jim's writing, probably igniting some indignation, but the words were never scratched out, remaining as a child's warm welcome for anyone who opens Mom's old Bible.

On the next page, again it's Jim who spells out "The Way of Salvation" with a verse for each of the five steps. Despite the inconsistent strokes of the preteen writer, the guidelines are there for all who want, as Jim points out in step three, a "way of escape."

Further scanning of the page showed several more of Mom's notes, countless underlining of promises pointing to heaven. The penciled marks had faded, and the inked jottings had bled through to other pages. But the evidence remained of carefully heard sermons and cherished hours alone with the Word.

In the back after concordance, guides, and maps, Mom listed several references to crown of joy, righteousness, life, and glory. First Thessalonians 2:19 reminded me again that Mom loved the thought of Christ's return.

On the last page, she again had written Psalm 37:4. It is framed by the doodling of youthful hands. One of the desires of Mom's heart was that her boys would grow up and do something useful and worthy with those hands. But her first desire, she told us, was that her four boys would make decisions to trust Christ. We have all done that.

Mom's old Bible reminds me of her hands—hands that held, spanked, mended, wiped tears, and produced a magic knot in the shoelaces on my three-year-old feet. Her hands turned the pages of that Bible for me until I learned to read it for myself.

Mother delighted herself in the Lord all her life, a continual encouragement to do something constructive with the hands that scribbled in her Bible so many years ago.

A Celebration Heart

by

KAREN BALL,
DAUGHTER, EDITOR, AUTHOR

There are a million memories I have of my mother—pastor's wife, mother, teacher's aide, camp cook, craft instructor, referee (between my brothers and me), encourager, disciplinarian, and the anchor of our family.

She taught me the value of celebration. She's always had a heart that makes every occasion in life into something special. Holidays, birthdays, events of every shape and kind were treated with equal enthusiasm and delight. And laughter, lots of laughter.

Valentine's Day saw the table set with everything red, from plates and napkins to food and drink. St. Patrick's Day was a festival of green. Whatever the celebration we found little gifts by our plates, just to remind us how special we were. Easter was a masterpiece of specially prepared eggs and baskets, carefully hidden baskets.

Christmas turned out to be a month-long celebration, complete with singing, decorations, cookies, and other special foods, along with "shopping night" when Mom took each of us out to shop, including dinner at a restaurant of our choice. I can still taste those milkshakes from Newberry's, so much better because I got to sit at the counter to drink it.

Any time our family gets together these days, the rooms ring with laughter as we remember those times. Whenever a holiday or special event approaches, I find myself nearly giddy with anticipation. When I was living two thousand miles away, I decided to pass along my mom's legacy. I invited friends from our Bible study and work to a Valentine's dinner, all set up just as Mom had done. What a delight to see our friends' eyes light up, to watch them enter into the spirit of the occasion, and to know I was sharing a bit of my mother with them.

One of those friends, after years of listening to me regale her with accounts of my wonderful parents and childhood, went with me to visit my home in Oregon. She was secretly convinced my memories must have become exaggerated over time—no one, she later told me, could be as great as I described my mom and dad.

Within a day, this friend said with her eyes wide, head shaking, "They really are the way you said!"

As a child I never would have understood her amazement. I thought everyone's mom was just like mine. The end of my school day was a favorite time when I would perch on the counter and recount the day's events as she fixed dinner. She listened and laughed with me, exclaimed over my latest poem or story or masterpiece of artwork. She did discipline when necessary but always with strong love mixed in. She played innumerable games with us, never letting us win but never minding when we did. She showed us every day the reality of a life dedicated to God, a heart submitting to his leading. She was a Christian who treated faith as a verb, not as some idealistic theory.

As an adult, now I realize how truly rare and special my mother was. Until her passing a few years ago, she was one of my closest friends, the one to share my day with, whose smiles, hugs, and laughter always blessed and encouraged me. She truly was a woman of God, servant, wife, and mother.

My mom, a special gift from God.

A Mother's Miracle

by

DANA ELWELL LAHON, MOTHER

Thursday, May 28, 1998, was just like any other day at my Florida home. Though the weather hadn't really warmed up yet, Brooke, my seven-year-old, and her best friend wanted to go swimming. I babysat infants during the day, so I couldn't be with them, but both of them are good swimmers.

My three-year old, Lacey, wanted to swim too. I was reluctant but decided she'd be okay with her big sister. I pulled up all the blinds at the window so I could keep an eye on the children while taking care of the babies.

In the midst of their fun, Lacey took off her flotation device and went down the slide. She sank straight to the bottom. Brooke and Julia were on the other side of the pool and didn't see her. No one knows how long she was underwater, but when Brooke *did* see her, she swam over immediately. She couldn't at first lift Lacey from the bottom, but finally in an adrenaline rush Brooke pulled her sister up by both arms and started screaming.

From inside I heard the commotion and realized something was wrong. I ran out and saw Lacey lying there, blue and lifeless. I stood frozen for a moment, then looked at Brooke, and she ran inside to call 911.

I am so thankful to God that I had taken CPR training for my childcare business. Lacey was so blue I was frantic. But I kept pushing and breathing until the emergency medical technicians arrived.

While I was working on her and waiting for help, I was crying out to God. *Please help me! God, please help!* That's when I heard a faint moan. I looked down at my daughter, then the sound of the ambulance.

The EMTs began working on her immediately, pumping and breathing life into my dying child, but nothing they did brought her back to consciousness. One of them said, "We've got to get her out of here now!" While I watched in horror, they took my baby into the back of the ambulance.

My husband, Mike, pulled up just then, and they told him there had been a drowning. When he looked into the ambulance and saw our daughter, his knees buckled and he fell to the road. One of the technicians radioed the hospital that they were coming in with a drowning victim, DOA. But before it had gone half a block, one of the medics opened the back door and hollered for Mike to meet them at the hospital—Lacey had awakened!

At the hospital they ran brain scans and lung tests, and each came back normal. When our little girl woke up the next morning in ICU and asked me to fix her hair, I knew God had given her back to us.

Besides the other miracle of a seven-year-old rescuing her sister, another was when the ambulance arrived at our house and found the front door locked. An EMT ran back to get an ax, but when he returned, the front door stood open. The only ones in the house at the time were by daycare babies.

I know God is sovereign and doesn't always work exactly as we ask him to. But having seen his miracles that day, I know I can trust him in all things.

And to All a Good Night

by

JERRY B. JENKINS,
SON AND AUTHOR

After Christmas many years ago, three elementary-school brothers played with their new toys until they were tired of them—about three days later.

Their mother brought an empty cardboard box into the dining room, sat the three down, and talked about underprivileged boys at a local orphanage who each got a piece of fruit, a candy bar, a comb, and a cheap toy.

"Merry Christmas," one of them said with a bit of sarcasm.

Their mother nodded, brows arched. "How about we give some of those kids a Christmas they won't forget?" They sat silent. She continued, "Let's fill this box with toys that will make their Christmas special. We'll do what Jesus would do."

One of the brothers had an idea. "With all my new stuff, I don't need all my old stuff!" He ran to get armloads of dingy, dilapidated toys, but when he returned his mother's expression stopped him.

"Is that what Jesus would do?"

He pursed his lips and shrugged. "You want us to give our new stuff?"

"It's just a suggestion."

"All of it?"

"I didn't have in mind all of it—just whatever you think."

"I'll give this car," one said, placing it in the box.

"If you don't want it, I'll take it," another said, reaching for it.

"I'm not givin' it to you—I'm givin' it to the orphans!"

"I'm done with this bow and arrow set," one offered.

"I'll take that," a brother chimed in. "I'll trade you these pens for that model."

"No deal. But I'll take the pens and that cap gun."

The boys hardly noticed their mother leave the room. The box sat there, its silent message unmistakable. The boys idly slipped away to play. But there was none of the usual laughing, arguing, rough-housing. Each with renewed vigor played with his favorite toys.

Eventually, one by one, the boys visited the kitchen in the small house, the only place their mother would be.

She was sitting at the table, her coat and hat and gloves on, and her expression looked like she was fighting tears. No words were exchanged. She was not going to browbeat her sons, no guilt trips, no pressure. Each returned to play quietly.

And then their mother came for the box. The oldest had carefully and resolutely placed almost all his new toys in it. The others selected more carefully but chose the best for the box.

Their mother took the box to the car without a word, an expression or gesture. She never reported on the reception by the orphans, and she was never asked.

Several years of childhood remained, but childhood selfishness had been dealt a blow.

One Brilliant Show

by

DAVID RUPERT, NATIONAL CHAPLAIN, POSTMASTERS OF AMERICA

Flowers—mom has always had a passion for them. She believed they could brighten any room, liven any conversation, and change any dour mood. As the flower coordinator at the First Baptist Church, she turned the plain wood altar in the front to a dazzling display of God's creation.

A negligible budget only provoked my resourceful mother's creativity. Every Saturday we searched the mountain countryside for willows and lilacs and wildflowers. Old dirt toads, creek beds, even abandoned graveyards were sources for colorful arrangements. The cold winters limited our natural flower habitat, so Mom utilized her dried collections pulled from boxes stacked high in the garage. Her delightful displays, no matter the season, often provided the subject for conversations after church—sometimes even more so than the sermon.

During the winter, Mom raised daffodils in pots lining her kitchen window—carefully watering, fertilizing, protecting, all in preparation for one brilliant exhibit at the altar. She chose an early spring day when the snow was still deep but the sun brilliant. The daffodil shoots were full and ready to burst, their tops still wrapped tight in the leafy envelope, when she picked them.

She placed the buds in a simple glass vase full of warm water, placing it at the front of the church hours before anyone else had arrived. I was concerned that the buds were still tightly wound, but her beguiling smile told me not to be concerned.

The congregants traipsed under overflowing gutters and slushy sidewalks, ducking streaming icicles from the roof edge as they entered the sanctuary. The service began as always with announcements and welcomes to visitors. Almost imperceptibly at first, then with amazing speed the buds began to open. By the time the sermon was over, the daffodils had exploded into panoply of color in praise to God.

After all these years, I have come to realize Mom raised her children much like those daffodils. Many times we thought we were overprotected, sheltered, prevented from "fun" like our friends. But she was preparing for us to bloom where we were planted, and at the right time she placed her children on the altar, an offering to her Maker.

Heavenly Cloth

by

LINDA WINDSOR,
MOTHER AND AUTHOR

Not all mothers are cut from the same cloth, but I believe all the cloth is made in heaven.

My mom never baked cookies or acted like a TV mother—or like anyone else's mom for that matter. Unable to find a Mother's Day card that really fit her, I modified one of a mom in a dress, apron, and holding a huge bouquet of flowers, obviously home-grown. I cut out a man's cap from a woodworkers catalog along with tools that I inserted in the bouquet—paintbrushes, pliers, pruning shears, etc. I hung a sander from her apron. Now *that* looked more like her—though I should have done away with the dress for jeans and one of those leather aprons with lots of pockets for tools. Just try to find a card with a mom dressed like that!

Without home-baked cookies or the luxury of having her there after school, much less help with homework, I learned how to tackle home projects and business assignments without intimidation. She's been there for every one I've tackled, often commandeering the crew. She taught me to be independent, to think for myself, and that nothing is impossible with God on my side.

She is not just my mother. She is my best friend and mentor. I have her to thank for who I am and what I am—for teaching me to dare to dream.

Dear Mom

by

LORI COPELAND, MOTHER AND AUTHOR

It's been thirty-three years now since you went to be with the Lord. How joyful your new life must be! I was a young woman when you left us that rainy morning in May, so we never really got to have a woman-to-woman talk like so many moms and daughters enjoy. I was barely able to comprehend the meaning of life, let alone the hole your passing would leave in my heart. Today, having raised three children of my own, I know a little more about a mother's love.

Those last few hours you opened your eyes with a soft litany of "I love you, I love you, I love you." Well, Mom, I loved you too. And I didn't tell you that nearly enough. I didn't thank you sufficiently for the multitude of ways that you expressed your love for me. Remember that special doll we argued over? A childish extravagance I thought I'd die if I didn't get. You did buy the doll, knowing you'd have to skimp on necessities the following week. You skimped often for your children. Thank you.

Thank you for your unconditional love during those times I was unlovable. For taking me to Sunday school and church every Sunday, teaching me the Lord is the Way, the Truth, the Life. Such richness all that has brought to my life.

Thank you for your night shift in a paper-cup factory, providing clothes, food, a roof over our heads. For your long walks home at two in the morning, pelting rain and blowing snowstorms keeping the car from climbing the rutted hill to our house. Those solitary treks must have been scary and lonely, and I thank you, Mom.

You were just fifteen when you married Dad. Your childhood wasn't the best, and you wanted to make sure your children's were better. Well, you and Dad accomplished that goal.

Your little chicks have grown into responsible adults—no one's been in jail yet. (A little humor there, Mom. I know you appreciate humor because what I remember most about you was your friendly smile which you gave to everyone.)

Thanks for circuses, movies on Saturday afternoons, and for that mouth-watering cocoa fudge you made very Sunday night. I can taste it to this day—creamy warm chocolate, rich black walnuts, with a generous dollop of real butter. I can still see you standing at the stove and stirring the candy to a boil, then testing it in a cup of cold water till it formed a perfect soft ball.

Thanks for leaving the porch light on until I was safely home.

I really do miss you, Mom. Over the years I realize the importance of having a mother at any age. Cancer is still an ugly blight on this earth, and hopefully the disease will one day be eradicated.

Mother's Day is coming. We buried you on Mother's Day. Still, every May I honor you in my heart and know that you are in heaven with God. How could I wish for more?

This Mother's Day I wanted to share a few thoughts I had not voiced while you were still with me. And to say thanks, Josephine Alice Smart, for giving me life and for teaching me that each new day is a gift from God, a wondrous bequest to be treasured. I'll see you one day soon, Mom. Keep the porch light on.

Your loving daughter, Lori

A Life That Mattered

by

ANNIE JONES,
MOTHER AND AUTHOR

My mom grew up poor in everything but faith, love, and laughter—those she knew in abundance and shared freely. She contracted polio when she was young and suffered with a lung condition exacerbated by growing up during the Depression in the Dust Bowl.

My mother did nothing particularly heroic in her life, yet every day of her life required heroic effort. Along with her other disabilities, she was diagnosed with rheumatoid arthritis in her twenties, and she lived in pain almost every day of her last fifty years. But she was a den mother, friend, confidante, working woman, and volunteer for everything from band fund raisers to comforting ICU patients' families. She ran her own business for a time, then became a single parent in her early fifties when her husband died. She lost six babies, but it did not make her bitter—it just made those of us who survived more precious. Fibrosis of the lungs was not helped by her smoking, and she had frequent bouts of pneumonia.

But she did not allow any of this to defeat her. Even in later years when she broke both hips, she was up weeks before her hip-replacement surgeons predicted. Her RA required joint replacement in both hands, but she still reached out to others. Mom was always on our side, no matter how stupid, stubborn, misguided, or selfish we were. She might not condone our actions, and she'd let us know when she disapproved, but we never doubted her love.

Her last days in the hospital saw her surrounded by three generations of women, all touched by her spirit in their own lives as they came one last time to say good-bye. We were determined she would not go into that long night alone, yet the mother in her would not surrender to the racking struggle for every breath as long as one of her children stood by.

To the end she was the best mother. There is so much more I could tell about her—the wisdom, humor, fairness. But maybe the highest praise is what I told her on her last day: Her life mattered.

I am better for having known her, having seen her faith in God, and having been loved by her gentle spirit. In turn the people my life touches will be better for what she instilled in me.

Mom's Garden

by

PEGGY M. WHITSON,
MOTHER AND AUTHOR

The image of my mother's garden
Brings peace into my soul.
But only after I touched each plan
Did I sense my spirit's growth.
Each dawn beyond the cornfields
A pink hue rises to meet the day.
God lifts the lily to greet the sunshine,
Baby robins come out to play.
I smile as I watch these wonders,
Knowing there was a time I didn't care.
Now as I pull tomatoes from the vines
I feel their beauty in a way I never dared.
Purring cats soak up each ray
Stretching idly while lapping the sun's kiss.

Gently squeezing off a raspberry, I think,
When I must go, it's not just Mom I'll miss.
The day has passed, so I take one last look,
Knowing the sun is due to set.
I realize tomorrow's a brand-new day
And God is not done with me yet.
Thank you, Mother, for your care,
For the gardens you have grown.
Not just on this land you worked
But in this heart that God now owns.

Time Capsule

by

MONA GANSBERG HODGSON,
MOTHER AND AUTHOR

What if I were to select three items for a time capsule that would symbolize my mother's role in my life? The first would be one of her flannel boards—a piece of cardboard covered with navy blue flannel and propped on an easel. In basement Sunday school rooms, my mother smoothed a background of a lion's den over the flannel and placed Daniel in jeopardy as he faced hungry lions. She would tell of Daniel's faithfulness to serve and trust God no matter the cost. She'd testify to the Lord's faithfulness to Daniel—and to us listening to the story.

Mom's songbook is next, *The Little Hymnal*—soft cover bright-blue book that traveled in Mom's purse. Rolling down the highway, Dad at the wheel, and eventually four daughters in the back seat, Mom would start a family sing-along. "Leaning on the Everlasting Arms," "Heavenly Sunshine," "When the Roll Is Called Up Yonder."

Mom was singing "The Lord is good, tell it wherever you go" over sudsy dishwasher when Dad's captain on the California Highway Patrol rang our doorbell with the news of an accident with Dad's patrol motorcycle. But four months of recovery and he was back on duty . . . in a patrol car.

Twenty-three years later, a lump of emotions caught in her throat, Mom sang "Turn Your Eyes upon Jesus" over Dad's deathbed. The truth was imprinted on her heart, along with the tradition of hymns to mark events.

A strand of pearls were known in our family as the wedding pearls. William Bert Gansberg, the man who would become my father, bought the pearls in Alaska at a Navy PX and presented them to his fiancée for Christmas, 1952. The white pearls adorned my mother's neck the next year when she walked down the aisle to become his bride.

Her granddaughters have begun a tradition of wearing the pearls at their weddings. The years have cast a shadow on their now golden patina, but like the family they encircle, they remain bound by a common thread.

Of course there are many other things that could symbolize Mother's role in my life. But these three have been significant training tools to mold and stretch my sensibilities.

A Grandmother Remembers Mama

by

DOROTHY SHELL BUNTING, DEBORAH BEDFORD'S GRANDMOTHER

Maurine, four when I was born, begged Mother to name me Dolly Dimples after the famous paper doll. Mother wrote this name in the family Bible, later changing it to Dolly Beatrice after persuading my sister I would not want "Dimples" after I was older. Then when I was old enough for school, Mother let me change the first name also, to Dorothy. So now I had a new grown-up name, Dorothy Beatrice.

In more recent memories, I see my mother at eighty-seven, living alone in our great old family home, strong and courageous, and of course, always loving. Yet my most precious memories are of her when I was a child and she was our young, beautiful mother. She sang to us, songs like "The Old Armchair" as she sat sewing at night after all the ironing and the dishes were done for the day, making clothes for the six children and shirts for Dad. And shirts for the good doctor, too, to reduce that ever-present medical bill.

I have a clear mental image of all of us standing in the front yard on a snowy Valentine's Day, watching her open the gate and walk to the mailbox. Slim and beautiful with black wavy hair pinned in a bun, she was wearing a bright red coat she had sewn for herself, and she turned to wave at us. That picture—a flash of scarlet against the snow—will always stay with me. She returned with a stack of envelopes, one for every one of her six children. We were thrilled to have gotten valentines, and too young to notice the envelopes had neither stamps nor postmarks.

Great Aunt Laura arrived at our house one Monday, shocked to find wash day occurring as usual. It had been widely predicted that the world was coming to an end this very day.

"Why, Lula," she said to Mother, "You shouldn't be washing clothes when the Lord comes!" Mother did not respond, simply continuing her scrubbing on the old washboard.

If he did come, their clothes would be clean.

Mother was interested in the news and what was happening in government and had a mind of her own, though she took no public positions. When the news came that women had been granted the right to vote, Dad hurried home at noon to tell her. I was in the kitchen with her when Dad came in and announced, "It has been passed—women have the right to vote!"

Mother stopped rolling the dough, wiped her hands on her apron and looked her astonishment at him.

"Oh, this is good," he told her. "I will be able to cast *two* votes now."

Mother was still looking at him. "That's what you think." Very softly she added, "I will choose the one I vote for."

World's Greatest Mom

by

JENNIFER LEE WHITT,
ROBIN LEE HATCHER'S
DAUGHTER

When my mother asked my sister and me to write a little piece on motherhood for this book, I promptly agreed. No problem. Yet all I have done since is ponder, and deadline is coming. . . .

"Done yet?" she wondered.

"I'm working on it, Mom," I said with a sigh.

I could happily reminisce for hours about my mother, especially about my childhood, but none of them describes how great she has always been at just that: being a mom. So I found myself staring at a blank computer screen, wondering how I could describe her worth to me.

Then I went to tuck my son into bed, kissing his cheek and whispering, "Sweet dreams," I remembered something I've heard since

238

my son was born—for me the ultimate compliment: "What a great mom you are."

I realized then that I am the best proof of what a wonderful mother I have. I have followed in her footsteps, continuing the tradition that my grandmother's grandmother began as I embarked on the road to becoming someone else's memories of . . .

The World's Greatest Mom.

My Mom

by

MICHAELYN J. HATCHER, ROBIN LEE HATCHER'S DAUGHTER

I was about eleven years old and attending a new school for the first time since kindergarten. I had never before gone to a school within walking distance, only riding a school bus several miles each way.

One lunch hour at my new school, one of the girls invited several of us to her house for lunch. It could be seen from the playground but a very tall fence stood in the way. Being active sixth graders, we just climbed over, went to her house, ate some lunch, played for a bit, and went back to school.

This time, waiting on the other side, were the principal and a teacher. And we were in big trouble. Leaving the grounds during school hours was against the rules. I hadn't known this and actually had walked home during lunch when I'd forgotten something.

But we were considered truants, and our parents were called. I had never been in trouble before, and I was scared and confused. When my mother came to pick me up, I told her what had happened and that the principal had threatened to spank all of us for our offense.

My mother was angry, and she said that before he could lay a hand on me he'd have to go through her first.

That's when I knew for sure Mom would always be there for me, and she always has.

I Love My Mama

by

AVERY BEDFORD, AGE 11 (WRITTEN IN 2001), DEBORAH BEDFORD'S DAUGHTER

I love my mama because . . .
She always helps me clean my room.
She makes good food for me to eat.
She stands up for me.
She give me *great* hugs and kisses.
She is not only my mom, but one of my best friends.
She went through lots of pain just to have me.
She always finds time to be with me.
She tries to act like a teenager to make me like her more.
She makes me tea when I get a sore throat.
She always gives me her true, honest answers.
I love my mom.

Creating Your Own Story Jar

by

DEBORAH BEDFORD &
ROBIN LEE HATCHER

After reading these tales of God's power and provision, both through fictional and real-life mothers, here are some ideas for creating your own story jars. It's actually quite simple, for use by an individual, a group of friends at a Bible study, or at a church.

Scripture encourages us to remember all God has done for us, and there is no more important arena for those memories than in the lives of our children. We all have special items, mementoes of places we've been, events we've experienced, miracles we've received from our loving Father.

Family times, such as Thanksgiving or Christmas dinners, offer a time and place to begin a story jar. Each participant can bring something to contribute to the jar, and as it drops in, tell what it means. We learn something new about loved ones when we hear their favorite or most meaningful memories in their own words.

This jar also provides a tool for remembering specific things God has done in our lives—miracles of transformation, of healing, of deliverance from evil of all kinds. Mrs. Halley, the pastor's wife in our stories, said that not all of God's miracles are in the Bible. He is still performing them today in countless ways both dramatic and gradual—changing lives, healing hearts.

If you have other ideas for creating a story jar, or if you would like to contact us about how this novel has impacted you or others in your life, we'd love to hear from you. Please contact us through our web sites.

Deborah and Robin
http://www.deborahbedfordbooks.com
http://www.robinleehatcher.com